KING ROTHER

UNIVERSITY OF NORTH CAROLINA
STUDIES IN THE GERMANIC LANGUAGES AND LITERATURES

Publication Committee

FREDERIC E. COENEN, EDITOR

WERNER P. FRIEDERICH   GEORGE S. LANE

JOHN G. KUNSTMANN   HERBERT W. REICHERT

11. Walter Silz. Realism and Reality: Studies in the German Novelle of Poetic Realism. 1954. Pp. xiv, 168. Paper $ 4.00.
12. Percy Matenko. LUDWIG TIECK AND AMERIKA: 1954.
13. Wilhelm Dilthey. THE ESSENCE OF PHILOSOPHY. Rendered into English by Stephen A. Emery and William T. Emery. 1954, 1961. Pp. xii, 78. Paper $ 1.50.
14. Edwin H. Zeydel and B. Q. Morgan. GREGORIUS. A. Medieval Oedipus Legend by Hartmann von Aue. Translated in Rhyming Couplets with Introduction and Notes. 1955. Pp. xii, 143. Paper $ 3.00.
15. Alfred G. Steer, Jr. GOETHE'S SOCIAL PHILOSOPHY AS REVEALED IN CAMPAGNE IN FRANKREICH AND BELAGERUNG VON MAINZ. With three full-page illustrations. 1955. Pp. xiv, 178. Paper $ 4.00.
16. Edwin H. Zeydel. GOETHE THE LYRIST. 100 Poems in New Translations facing the Original Texts. With a Biographical Introduction and an Appendix on Musical Settings. 1955. Pp. xviii, 182, 2nd. ed. 1958. Paper $ 1.75.
17. Hermann J. Weigand. THREE CHAPTERS ON COURTLY LOVE IN ARTHURIAN FRANCE AND GERMANY. Out of print.
18. George Fenwick Jones. WITTENWILER'S «RING» AND THE ANONYMOUS SCOTS POEM «COLKELBIE SOW». Two Comic-Didactic Works from the Fifteenth Century. Translated into English. With five illustrations. 1956. Pp. xiv, 246. Paper $ 4.50.
19. George C. Schoolfield. THE FIGURE OF THE MUSICIAN IN GERMAN LITERATURE. 1956. Out of print.
20. Edwin H. Zeydel. POEMS OF GOETHE. A Sequel to GOETHE THE LYRIST. New Translations facing the Originals. With an Introduction and a List of Musical Settings. 1957. Pp. xii, 126. Paper $ 3.25.
21. Joseph Mileck. HERMANN HESSE AND HIS CRITICS. The Criticism and Bibliography of Half a Century. 1958. Ont of print.
22. Ernest N. Kirrmann. DEATH AND THE PLOWMAN or THE BOHEMIAN PLOWMAN. A Disputatious and Consolatory Dialogue about Death from the Year 1400. Translated from the Modern German Version of Alois Bernt. 1958. Pp. xviii, 40. Paper $ 1.85.
23. Edwin H. Zeydel. RUODLIEB. THE EARLIEST COURTLY NOVEL (after 1050). Introduction, Text, Translation. Commentary, and Textual Notes. With seven illustrations. 1959. Pp. xii, 165. Paper $ 4.50.
24. John T. Krumpelmann. THE MAIDEN OF ORLEANS. A Romantic Tragedy in Five Acts by Friedrich Schiller. Translated into English in the Verse Forms of the Original German. 1959. Pp. xiv, 130. Paper $ 3.50.
25. George Fenwick Jones. HONOR IN GERMAN LITERATURE. 1959. Pp. xii, 208. Paper $ 4.50.
26. MIDDLE AGES—REFORMATION—VOLKSKUNDE. FESTSCHRIFT for John G. Kunstmann. Twenty Essays. 1959. Ont of print.
27. Martin Dyck. NOVALIS AND MATHEMATICS. 1960. Pp. xii, 109. Paper $ 3.50.
28. Claude Hill and Ralph Ley. THE DRAMA OF GERMAN EXPRESSIONISM. A German-English Bibliography. 1960. Pp. xii, 211. Paper $ 5.00.
29. George C. Schoolfield. THE GERMAN LYRIC OF THE BAROQUE IN ENGLISH TRANSLATION. 1961. Pp. x, 380. Paper $ 7.00. Cloth 8 50.
30. John Fitzell. THE HERMIT IN GERMAN LITERATURE. (From Lessing to Eichendorff.) 1961. Pp. xiv, 130. Paper $ 4.50. Cloth $ 6.00.
31. Heinrich von Kleist. THE BROKEN PITCHER. A Comedy. Translated into English Verse by B. Q. Morgan. 1961. Pp. x, 74. Paper $ 2.00.
32. Robert W. Linker. MUSIC OF THE MINNESINGERS AND EARLY MEISTERSINGERS. 1962. Pp. xvi, 79. Paper $ 2.00. Cloth $ 3.50.
33. Christian Reuter. SCHELMUFFSKY. Translated into English by Wayne Wonderly. 1962. Pp. xiv. 104. Paper $ 3.50. Cloth $ 5.00.
34. Werner A. Mueller. THE NIBELUNGENLIED TODAY. 1962. Pp. xi, 99. Paper $ 2.50. Cloth $ 4.00.
35. F. C. Richardson. KLEIST IN FRANCE. 1962. Pp. xii, 210. Paper $ 5.00. Cloth $ 6.50.
36. Robert Lichtenstein. KING ROTHER. Translated from the German. With an Introduction. 1962. P. xviii, 120. Paper $ 4.00. Cloth $ 5.50.

Foreign Sales through:
Librairie E. Droz
8 Rue Verdaine
Geneva, Switzerland

NUMBER THIRTY-SIX

UNIVERSITY
OF NORTH CAROLINA
STUDIES IN
THE GERMANIC LANGUAGES
AND LITERATURES

KING ROTHER

Translated By

ROBERT LICHTENSTEIN

CHAPEL HILL
THE UNIVERSITY OF NORTH CAROLINA PRESS

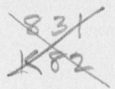

Printed in Spain   **Impreso y hecho en España**

Depósito Legal: V. 1.926-1962

Tipografía Moderna, Valencia, Spain, 1962

INTRODUCTION

Written some time around 1160, *König Rother* is the oldest example in German of the secular epic, the first long narrative poem in the vernacular to have come down to us which seeks, not to instruct or to edify, but simply to entertain. Its appearance marks a turning point in the course of German literature.

During the preceding hundred years, poetry —written poetry, that is— had been completely subservient to the interests of the Church. Ever since, around 1060, the cold wind of monastic reform, emanating from the West, had begun to sweep across the German lands, clerics had been sedulously at work versifying all manner of religious materials —sermons, legends, articles of faith, paraphrases of the Bible, summonses to repentance. With little regard for the formal requirements of the medium, they had taught, admonished, and exhorted —all to the end of man's eternal redemption. In crudely built couplets they had sung of the sinfulness of the flesh, the vanity of worldly things, the overwhelming need for repentance. This earthly abode they had depicted as a brief resting-place, a temporary station on man's journey to his ultimate destination, full of snares and pitfalls, devoid of all positive values. Contempt for the world —that was the single theme on which they had rung countless changes.

Such a drastic limitation upon the scope of literature could, of course, endure only as long as the ascetic world-view of the Church went unchallenged among all classes of the population. By the middle of the twelfth century it had become clear that this was no longer the case. A new culture, with its own values and ideals, had emerged to compete with the old hieratic order for power and influence. This new culture we characterize as "courtly" because the climate most conducive to its flourishing prevailed at the courts of the great nobles. There the exponents of the new cultural values gathered, the members of the knightly class, whose social standing had recently been strengthened by their participation in the Crusades. Acknowledging the possession of God's grace as the greatest good, they were yet not disposed to forgo the pleasures and satisfactions of this world. Elegant manners, fine raiment, a handsome bearing, glory earned upon the battlefield or in the tourney, the approbation of the ladies —these stood high among the things they valued; and these were the things they wished to see reflected in a new kind of literature, a secular literature.

So far as we know, the first one who addressed himself to the task of writing for this new public was the author of *König Rother*. Realizing that, if his work were to succeed, it would have to contribute to the festive spirit of the court, he put together a story of intrigue and adventure, peopled it with doughty knights and beautiful ladies, set it against a splendid background, embellished it with lavish descriptions of material wealth, and made sure to include festivals and tournaments and the ceremonial of the court. When he was done, he had written the first tale of romantic adventure for the entertainment of a courtly audience.

Who was the author of this truly novel and significant work? The poet's name we shall never know: he chose to remain anonymous. Concerning his station in life, it was at one time popular to picture him as a *Spielmann*, a minstrel; only such a one, it was felt, could have written those scenes of low comedy in which the principal actors are a band of uncouth giants. On stylistic grounds, too, one thought one could detect the hand of the minstrel. Today this theory no longer convinces. The burlesque humor in which the poem abounds may well have been present already in the popular sources upon which the poet drew. And the stylistic features —the crudities and exaggerations, the stereotyped phrases and the stock epithets— are also part of that same oral tradition from which the poem sprang. (That the authors or transmitters of the oral sources of *König Rother* may have been minstrels is not at all improbable). Today it seems more likely that the poet's profession is more truly revealed by the pious note which, struck from time to time in the course of the poem, becomes especially loud towards the close when, having finished with his sources, he felt freer to indulge the promptings of his own spirit. In all probability, the poet was a cleric, an open-minded man who liked to listen to the stories and songs popular among the people and felt it a beguiling task to adapt such material to the taste of his noble patrons. The dialect in which he wrote, as well as references to local saints, indicate that he came from the Rhineland. That his audience was to be found among aristocratic circles in Bavaria is the conclusion to be drawn from the fact that some of the figures in his tale bear the names of noble Bavarian families.

What were the poet's sources? How much did he owe to material already at his disposal? From the evidence we have, it seems that he was familiar with two short pieces of oral poetry, two ballads, both of which were built upon the widespread motif of the abduction of a princess; and that he set to work when he saw how the two could be easily joined together to provide the outlines of a long narrative poem of the sort already popular in France.

It is possible to reconstruct the main lines of the first ballad if we compare the version of it in *König Rother* with the much shorter and simpler version which is found in that collection of heroic legends known as the *Thidrekssaga*. From such a comparison it seems that the original ballad went about as follows: A young king, unmarried but eager to wed, is informed of the whereabouts of a beautiful princess. At once he dispatches twelve of his men to woo her for him. The princess' father, who considers no one to be worthy of his daughter, has the envoys thrown into a dungeon. After a year has gone by without news of his men, the young king sets out with a company of his knights to rescue them; he takes along some giants too, among whom are Asprian and Widolt with the Iron Club. Arriving in the land of the unfriendly king, he gives himself out as a banished nobleman named Dietrich. Summoned into the presence of the king, he kneels at his feet and pleads to be taken into his service. While he does so, the giants carry on in such a way that the king, intimidated, reluctantly accepts his offer. Dietrich's generosity wins him great popularity among the people, and many knights flock to his side. The princess, hearing of the splendid stranger, becomes enamored of him. Dietrich brings about a meeting by sending the princess two shoes, one of gold and one of silver. When she tries them on, she finds to her dismay that they both fit the same foot. At her request Dietrich comes to her apartment with the shoes for the other foot. Kneeling before her, he reveals to her his true identity. She agrees to flee with him. But first arrangements must be made to rescue the envoys. The princess persuades her father to release them from the dungeon for three days against Dietrich's surety. While they are at large, a tunnel is secretly built from the dungeon up to the surface of the earth. The envoys are returned to the dungeon. One night the plan of escape is carried out. The young king flees with the princess and all his men. With an army the old king rides in pursuit. In the battle that follows he is defeated. A reconciliation takes place and the young king brings his bride safely home.

So may the groundwork for the first half of the poem have appeared. What changes did the poet see fit to make? First of all, he transferred the setting to the Eastern Mediterranean. The young king, now called Rother, becomes the Roman Emperor; his residence is at Bari. The princess' father is transformed into the Byzantine Emperor Constantine. (These changes may have been suggested by a recent event. In the years 1143/44 Roger II, the Norman King of Sicily, had unsuccessfully sought to bring about a marriage between his son and the daughter of the Emperor Manuel. The envoys whom he had sent to the court at Constantinople were imprisoned.) The new locale made possible the introduction of a new figure - Ymelot, a heathen king. He makes his entrance soon after the envoys have been returned to their dungeon. With a mighty host he invades Constantine's realm. As a result, the prisoners (who, in the original ballad, had been freed by cunning) are released by Constantine so that they may help Rother, who has offered his services in defending the realm against the infidels. At the head of his men, Rother rides forth with Constantine and his army to meet the advancing foe. By a show of great prowess Rother captures Ymelot. He is sent back to Constantinople ahead of the host that he may announce the good tidings. Arriving in the city, he pretends that he has been forced to flee before the victorious heathens. He persuades the princess to take refuge upon his ship, whereupon he sails away with her to Bari.

For the second half of his poem the poet has used a ballad based upon a Hebraic-Byzantine legend which had grown up around the figure of King Solomon. (This ballad was later to be expanded into the poem entitled *Salman und Morolf*, of which the only version we have was written around 1300.) With this ballad *König Rother* shares the following incidents: A minstrel in the service of a king (Pharaoh, Constantine) abducts the wife of another king (Solomon, Rother). The latter leads an expedition to win back his wife. Leaving his army just outside the town to which his wife has been taken, he proceeds into the town, disguised as a pilgrim. Stealthily he enters the palace in which his wife is being kept. He is discovered and condemned to death. One grants him his last wish: that he be hanged at a spot of his own choosing. (The spot is, of course, close by the place where his men are lying in wait.) Just as the sentence is about to be executed, he blows upon his horn, whereupon his army emerges from the wood and sets him free. In the ensuing battle his persecutors are slain. There follows a scene in which he is reunited with his wife.

Into the action of this second ballad the author of *König Rother* has introduced a new motif — that of the returning husband. Rother steals into the palace just as his wife is about to be forced to wed the son of Ymelot. (Ymelot, who had been taken captive in the first half of the poem, has since escaped and has returned to Constantinople with a mighty army. Constantine, forced to sue for peace, has offered his daughter in marriage to Ymelot's son.) Rother makes his presence known to his wife by means of a ring. Discovered doing so, he is taken captive, whereupon the events follow as related above. In the end Constantine is compelled to throw himself upon Rother's mercy. Magnanimously Rother spares his life, then sails home once more with his wife.

Having reached this point in his story, the poet might well have stopped. Twice had Rother got the better of Constantine. The second time he had forced him to submit unconditionally to his might. Here, surely, was a fitting conclusion to a poem whose basic theme was the contest for supremacy between the two mightiest rulers of the Christian world. But the poet felt that two things had still to be done: first, he had to place his work in a historical context; and second, he had to end on a properly edifying note.

To achieve his first aim, he has Rother's wife give birth to a son right after she has set foot upon Roman soil for the second time. The child, christened Pippin, is destined to become the father of Charles the Great. Such a genealogical connection, establishing as it did Rother's historical legitimation, secured the poem against the charge that it was a mere tissue of lies. At the same time, it cast back upon Rother some of the radiance which emanated from the great Carolingians.

The poem comes to an end with Rother's decision to quit the throne in favor of his son Pippin and to become a monk. This should not be interpreted as the poet's gesture of appeasement to the Church. In that age it was not at all unusual for a great nobleman to retire from the world. Besides, it gave the final touch to the portrait of Rother as the ideal Christian king.

On the whole, it must be agreed that the poet has made excellent use of the opportunities for epic expansion afforded him by his sources. Scenes which in the ballads could have been only lightly sketched in, he has drawn with firmer contours, filled with local color, and enveloped with the atmosphere of real life. Here in *König Rother*, for the first time in German literature, something has been captured of the contemporary world. Here is the life of the court in all its pomp and splendor; here are the celebrations and the ceremonial, the fine apparel and the shining armor, the lovely ladies and the doughty knights. But here, too, is a darker side of that life. In the dungeon scenes the poet has not shunned to give a graphic picture of human misery. Truly moving is the episode in which the prisoners emerge blinking into the light of day, feeble and emaciated after their long captivity, while their relatives and friends stand around seeking to suppress any sign of emotion lest thereby they reveal their true identities. It is in such scenes that the poet has convincingly demonstrated his mastery of the epic technique.

Although the characters have been conceived as types rather than as individuals, some of them come remarkably alive: one thinks especially of the three women of the story — the sharp-tongued old queen, the resolute princess, and the enterprising lady-in-waiting. The two protagonists, Rother and Constantine, stand out in bolder relief by reason of their dramatic contrast.

Rother is the very pattern of princely excellence. Unsurpassed in wealth and power, he presides over a court that is famous for its splendid and decorous ways. His conduct is at all times befitting to one so highly stationed: not even in the most trying situations does he lose his composure. Prudent and resourceful, he well deserves his reputation as "the astute man." The loyalty which binds him to his followers is absolute. His generosity to those who have deserved well of him is unbounded. He has compassion for the weak and the needy. He lacks the spirit of vengefulness and strives after justice. His deepest wish is to make himself pleasing in the sight of God. He is in truth an exemplary Christian monarch.

As Rother is the *rex justus*, so Constantine is the *rex injustus*. In him have been embodied all the repugnant features of the Byzantine emperor as he was seen by the Crusaders. He is vain and cowardly He alienates his followers by his stinginess. He is lacking in dignity and self-control. But his greatest sin is that of *superbia*, pride. How, he wants to know, does anyone dare to invade his realm? And yet he proves himself unable to cope with the theat posed by the infidels. In the end he is forced to submit to Rother, to repent his ways, and to promise that henceforth he will dedicate himself to a life of good works. Rother's triumph over Constantine symbolizes the supremacy of Rome over Byzantium.

The style of *König Rother* shows many resemblances to that of oral poetry. The story is told in a swift and straightforward way; there are very few poetic figures, and edifying excursions occur only towards the end. The sentence structure is predominantly paratactic. Stock phrases and epithets abound. The poet lays great stress upon keeping in close contact with his audience: he addresses it directly, assures it of the truth of what it is hearing, comments upon some interesting moment in the narrative. Frequently he gives vent to his feelings in exclamations of wonder or dismay. It is this colloquial tone which is responsible for much of the fresh and spirited effect of *König Rother*; and it is this tone which I have done my utmost to capture in my translation. I have tried to keep archaic and other unusual expressions to a minimum. Always I have been concerned not to depart from the normal English word order. (Inversions, which are so incompatible with a colloquial style, I have, with few exceptions, allowed only at the end of a line when it was the case of a stock epithet, as in *lady fair* or *hero true*.)

In two important ways does the style of my translation differ from that of the original. I have allowed myself much less latitude with respect to impure rhymes; and I have employed a more regular meter by avoiding the clash of two stressed syllables coming directly one upon the other. These two departures I felt it necessary to adopt in the interest of readability. Rhymes and rhythms which public taste had already rejected in the thirteenth century as being too crude and archaic would have fallen with intolerable harshness upon modern ears — even upon such as are accustomed to the most dissonant effects of our contemporary poets.

The verses of the translation have been numbered to facilitate comparison with the original. The text used is that of Frings and Kuhnt (Halle: Max Niemeyer Verlag, 1954), which lists the literature on *König Rother* starting with the year 1922. For literature up to 1922 one should consult the Frings-Kuhnt edition of that year. The interested reader will find excellent discussions of the poem in the standard histories of Ehrismann, Fr. Vogt, Schwietering, H. Schneider, and de Boor.

KING ROTHER

    Upon the shore of the Western Sea
There lived a lord of high degree.
Rother was the hero's name,
And he resided rich in fame
5 There at Bari in the town.
Before him other lords knelt down,
Princes seventy-and-two,
Honorable men and true:
To him was subject all their land.
10 He was the most illustrious man
Who ever sat upon the throne
And governed in the town of Rome.
   Rother was a mighty king.
Splendidly went everything
15 And very decorously at his court
(If we can judge from our report),
So that he lacked nothing in his life
Except that he was without a wife.
Then the young counts all with one accord
20 Wished to hear from their noble lord
Why they should go on tilling their land
As long as he was a single man.
They held that it was only right
That if one was a worthy knight
25 And a ruler over the whole domain
And over so many a well-born thane,
Then he ought to take to himself a spouse
To be and adornment to his house,
For if he died without an heir,
30 Then they were sure to die of despair:
Whom should they then seat on the throne
To govern in the town of Rome?
   Thus did the noble lord reply:

L. 1 *the Western Sea* — the Adriatic.
L. 5 *Bari* — a seaport in Apulia (southern Italy).
L. 7 *seventy-and-two* — the use of numbers in this way is a characteristic feature of the popular epic style.

"Very much afraid am I
35 That if a princess I did take
And it turned out to be a mistake,
Then I would have to pay with my head.
A well-born maiden I'd gladly wed,
A lady of such high degree
40 That she might suit a king like me
And over my proudest dukes might reign.
But I don't know of one in my whole domain
Who pleases me so fully
That you could praise her truly."
45   Now a count was among his retinue
Who helped him with his counsel true
So that much glory came to him:
Thus did he serve his sovereign.
(Into dire distress he later came.)
50 Lupold was the hero's name,
And at Rother's court he had been raised
With the greatest care in his younger days.
He was his vassal and his kin,
And for counsel Rother turned to him.
55 Never did a truer man
Serve the king of the Roman land.
From the midst of all the people then
There came together the worthiest men —
Noble lords both old and wise.
60 Honor above all they did prize,
And to decorum they paid heed.
Upon a maiden they agreed.
   Lupold spoke the first of all.
"By our Redeemer, I recall
65 That in the East across the sea
A great king's daughter lives splendidly
In Constantinople Town,
The citadel of great renown.
Constantine is the ruler there.
70 His daughter is a maiden fair.
From her retinue she shines afar
As from the heavens the morning star.
She surpasses every other maid
As gold surpasses silk brocade.
75 She is so slender in the waist
That by her no lord would be disgraced.
And so lofty is her pedigree
That delighted by her a king might be.

One waits upon her constantly.
80 But this I swear by Almighty God,
To win her will be no easy job,
For whoever has tried to make her his wife
Has had to pay for it with his life!"
   To Rother it was told anon
85 What counsel had been agreed upon.
Then he asked a count to tell him plain
(Herman was the gentleman's name)
Whom he should send across the sea
To woo him the maiden faithfully.
90 Thus did the margrave make reply:
"Upon my counsel you can rely.
Lupold, sire, is the man to go!
With all his heart he loves you so,
And he knows how things stand with the maiden fair.
95 Such is my counsel, I declare!
If you can in a friendly way
Persuade the noble lord to say
That your ambassador he will be,
He will woo you the maiden most faithfully."
100   Quickly Rother sent his men
And summoned Lupold to him then.
When he came before his sovereign,
A courteous welcome was given to him.
Up from his chair the margrave sprang
105 In accordance with his lord's command.
As soon as Lupold took his seat,
Rother politely began to speak.
"It is on account of my grievous plight
That I have sent for you, good knight.
110 I wish you to woo the maid for me
Who so wondrous fair is said to be:
Thereby you will help me enhance my name.
In truth, these gentlemen all maintain
That you are the very one to go.
115 For the sake of your honor you can't say no!"
   Thus did Lupold answer him
(He dearly loved his sovereign):
"Sire, such urging need not be.
Your honor is so dear to me
120 That I pledge to do this thing for you
As faithfully as I'm able to,
And win the hand of the maiden fair —
Or else my life I will forswear.

      Now summon to the court such men
125 As you may well be able to send
      In accordance with propriety
      To a country far across the sea:
      Eleven counts of high degree;
      The twelfth one I myself shall be.
130 I wish moreover that each count bring
      Twelve comely knights along with him,
      All decked out in such array
      That a king may receive us without dismay."
        To the court King Rother summoned then
135 The proudest of his liegemen —
      Princes seventy-and-two.
      (They always rendered him service true.)
      As soon as he had disclosed his plan,
      Then up spoke many a valiant man:
140 "If you should order me, sire, to fare
      To the ends of the earth, I solemnly swear
      That I would very gladly go:
      Homage to you we all do owe."
      Then eleven counts swore to their king
145 That they would woo the maid for him.
      They loved him truly, so we're told,
      On account of the silver and the gold
      Which he gave to them so royally.
      They discharged their mission loyally.
150   As soon as their word was plighted,
      Then at the court was knighted
      A count (Erwin was his name).
      Thereupon the youthful thane
      Fitted out his warriors fair
155 With skins of sable and of vair.
      The other nobles followed suit:
      Handsomely each equipped his troop.
      They mounted steeds that were snowy white.
      So many envoys well-bedight
160 Were never seen in any land.
      They were led by a very prudent man.
      He was cherished dearly by the king,
      And had never done a dishonest thing.
        The ships were loaded without delay.
165 Lupold wished to sail away.
      Rother bade him not to depart
      And sent a man to fetch his harp.
      He had devised a clever sign

Which he was to use at a later time.
170 He ordered the noblemen to go
And stand on deck all in a row.
Three melodies he played thereon
Which they did recognize later on.
Then to them all the good lord said:
175 "If you are ever sore bestead
And these three tunes you happen to hear,
You can be sure that I am near!"
This gladdened the heart of many a knight
Who later was in a sorry plight.
180 In song they raised their voices high
And journeyed forth beneath the sky.
Ah, how the swelling sails did gleam
As they went sailing with the stream.
    The nobles journeyed from the land.
185 Rother stood upon the strand
And prayed that Almighty God above,
In token of His lasting love,
Might deign to bring the gentlemen
Safely back to the realm again.
190 "If anyone then desires my gold
I'll give it to him in amounts untold.
But if castles and land he should prefer,
So much to him will I transfer
Until he's content with what he has won —
195 How gladly I'll see that that is done!
And I shall help him defend his land
With the help of this my trusty brand."
    The messengers of high degree
Journeyed far across the sea
200 To Constantinople in Greek domain.
Their vessels they did beach amain
There upon that foreign shore.
Knightly raiment each man wore,
Fashioned in identical wise.
205 Theirs was a hardy enterprise!
Lupold asked a merchant then
To watch their ships a while for them
Until from the court they should return:
A rich reward he would thereby earn.
210 In token thereof he gave him a cloak.
"For three full days," the merchant spoke,
"I'll keep an eye on your ships for you,
No matter where you wander to.

I swear by Almighty God on high,
215 Who fashioned me to live and die,
You've given to me so royally
That I'll guard your vessels loyally!"
　　The nobles dressed themselves so well
(As far as I am able to tell)
220 That never before to anyone
Did so many handsome envoys come.
Their cloaks were weighted to the ground
With the finest sapphires that could be found.
Dragons of the purest gold
225 Adorned the dress of the heroes bold;
And other creatures —hart and hind,
And marvelous things of every kind—
Were wrought in gold in their attire,
All in accordance with their desire.
230 Silks and satins made more dear
The bells upon their riding-gear.
(This earned for them much praise indeed.)
To the court in splendor they did proceed.
　　To Constantine's court the nobles came.
235 Then their steeds were led from them amain
Ah, how the sapphires flashed their fire
Back and forth in their attire!
The worthy Erwin did not delay:
He bade his twelve men make their way
240 After him decorously.
The other lords did the same as he:
Each went at the head of his own band.
How eagerly their dress was scanned!
Then to the king came a report
245 That there was present at his court
A company of warriors fair.
Ah, how many ran to stare
Who straightway then to the ladies pressed
To tell how the strangers all were dressed.
250 　　The goodly queen said thereupon:
"Constantine, rise up anon
And let us welcome these strangers here.
Dearly should I like to hear
From whence these gentlemen do fare.
255 Curious raiment they do wear!
Whosoever did command
That they should journey to our land
Must be a lord of considerable might —

If I am able to judge aright.
260 Sire, it would seem wise to me
To treat these envoys honorably.
Such an answer will not do
As you've made to so many hitherto.
Never, I think, did such a band
265 Journey so splendidly to this land.
All of them are fair to see—
Horse and rider equally!
Such a splendid troop, I ween,
In Constantine's realm was never seen."
270 To the court the Emperor hastened then
And greeted politely the noblemen.
Likewise did the goodly queen:
She welcomed there with courteous mien
Every one in like degree
275 And bowed to them decorously.
There rose up then a mighty press
As everyone marveled at their dress.
The gentlemen and the ladies fair
Only wanted to stand and stare.
280 Then up spoke Herlint, an ancient dame:
"That must be indeed a strange domain
From whence these gentlemen do fare.
So many sapphires they do wear
Set in gold most splendidly!
285 If only the good Lord would decree
That we might see the nobleman
Who sent these envoys to our land!"
    Then to the king did Lupold say:
"Give me your consent, I pray,
290 That I may complete without any fear
The errand which has brought me here.
Permit me, sire, to tell you true
What a mighty king proposes to you.
He is the handsomest man, I swear,
295 Who ever drew breath anywhere,
And he has a mighty following.
Doughty warriors serve the king.
There is great joy at my master's court.
One sees there falcons trained for sport,
300 Battle-steeds and damsels fair;
And knightly armor is also there,
Very much to my master's taste.
And so you will not be disgraced

If to my message you lend an ear.
305 As a knight my lord is without a peer."
    Constantine replied thereto:
"Now it shall be granted you,
Seeing you ask it for your sire.
Let me know what you desire.
310 You are a handsome lad indeed!
You have my permission to proceed."
Then Lupold said without more ado
(To Rother no one was more true):
"This, O King, is the word I bear:
315 My lord desires your daughter fair.
Rother is my master's name,
And he dwells in the West beyond the main.
He is a man of high esteem,
And he wants your daughter for his queen.
320 And should Almighty God decree
That joined together they may be,
Then never before will any wife
Have had with a man a better life."
    Sadly Constantine replied
325 (Truly, he was mortified):
"Now must I rue for many a week
That I permitted you to speak.
If I could find it in my heart
To allow my daughter to depart,
330 Then with my honor it might accord
To send her to your noble lord.
But by Almighty God I vow
That you were very shrewd just now
When you got permission to speak from me —
335 Else the light of day you'd nevermore see!
For whoever would take my daughter to wife
Has had to pay for it with his life.
Now though that's not your fate this time,
You all are prisoners of mine.
340 Here in my land you must remain
And never shall see your homes again!"
    Constantine had the envoys fair
Brought into a dungeon bare.
There they spent a weary time.
345 For them the sun did never shine,
Nor did the moon send down its light.
Too soon had pleasure taken flight!
Always they were wet and cold.

      Ah, their suffering can't be told!
350 Hungry were they and sore bestead;
      Often they were almost dead.
      They who at home had all they craved,
      In the water now were forced to bathe
      Which was flowing underneath them there.
355 How wretchedly did the nobles fare!
      Many a man then wept aloud
      To see the state of his body proud.
      Within their hearts great sorrow dwelt;
      To no one might they look for help.
360 And yet our gracious Lord above,
      In token of His lasting love,
      Saw that later they all came
      Safely back to their homes again.
         Hearken further to the plight
365 Of many a deserving knight!
      To Master Lupold then did say
      The noble Erwin in his dismay:
      "Woe is me, my brother dear!
      How much longer must we be here?
370 How long can our kinsmen live
      Without the aid we are pledged to give?
      Or tell me who will finally
      Inherit all our property.
      May God Almighty of His grace
375 Deliver us from this evil place!"
      They all fell crosswise to the ground.
      How loudly did their cries resound
      As they called out unto the Lord!
      How piteously they all implored!
380 How painfully their hearts did swell!
      Some of them into the water fell
      So that they never rose up again.
      But later for the other men
      There arrived a happy day
385 When to their homes they sailed away.
         Constantine then bade to him
      Both his vassals and his kin,
      And sent them to see the objects fair
      Which in the ships had been carried there.
390 Then many a damsel went apace
      Along with the others to the place
      Where the mighty treasure was known to be,
      To see what marvels she might see.

Now truly, one would try in vain
395 To tell all the wonders the ships contained.
The ruddy gold was stored therein,
Stretched to wire extremely thin.
Brooches were there and fingerrings,
Along with many other things
400 Which the envoys had brought for the ladies fair.
Five thousand armlets, too, were there
Which they had planned to give away
Whenever they should end their stay.
Horses' blankets and pennons gay
405 Were lying there in great array.
Elegant tents could one behold,
Artfully adorned with gold,
Given to them by their kinsmen dear
When from the country they should steer,
410 And which they had chosen for their own.
At that time had sailed across the foam
Many a lad with spirits high —
In case our story does not lie.
   Now you can hear more about gold and treasure!
415 If to see great wealth was anyone's pleasure,
There was enough of it on display.
Constantine had it carried away
And given into his treasurer's care.
And he told him that he should beware
420 Lest ever there should be a lack
In case one wanted anything back.
Be it armor or pennons gay,
Not a thing must go astray!
And if a courser were to die,
425 Another one he must supply —
Else with his life he would have to pay.
And he bade him guard it in such a way
That if it were given back again,
Nothing should be missing then.
430   Now a year and a day had passed
Since first those warriors were cast
Into that prison beneath the ground.
Great travail the poor men found.
Never did they cease to moan.
435 And also Rother back at home
Bitterly wept both day and night
On account of so many a worthy knight.
He wrung his hands in his dismay

And kept on thinking night and day
440 How without danger he might detect
Where the envoys were being kept.
Then all the wise old counselors came
Whose kinsmen had sailed across the main.
Many a bitter tear they shed
445 And with their gracious lord they pled
That he himself should go and see
Whether alive they still might be.
   Rother sat upon a stone;
From his heart all joy had flown.
450 For three full days he neither stirred
Nor spoke to anyone a word
But kept on thinking night and day
Whether there might be some way
Of getting to that doughty band
455 Who had ventured forth at his command
To the land of Greece beyond the main.
Then he summoned Berchter, an ancient thane,
To advise him what he ought to do.
He always gave him counsel true.
460 (Seven of his sons on that trip had gone,
And he could always be counted on.)
The king said: "Berchter, counsel me
How I can come across the sea
To Constantinople with my men.
465 I swear that if it turns out then
That God has permitted Constantine
To slay those messengers of mine,
Then nevermore shall I be found
Anywhere on Roman ground
470 Until with his own life he has paid.
Ah, how wretched I have been made!"
   To him said Berchter, that ancient man
(He was, in truth, a count of Meran):
"Eleven splendid sons I had.
475 The twelfth was Helfrich, a doughty lad.
He ventured forth at your command
Across the Elbe with a mighty band.
There he led his men to war.
Always he was to the fore
480 The time he slew the heathen horde
Who would not recognize our Lord.

L. 473 *Meran* — Dalmatia.

In God's employ he has been slain.
His death must give us lasting pain.
Now seven sons on this trip did go
485 For whom I shall always suffer so.
From now on I must live forlorn.
Ah, would that I had never been born!
Lupold was my eldest son,
And after him did Erwin come.
490 Now though I don't mention the other five,
For these two my grief will be always alive.
Rother, lord and master dear,
To my counsel lend an ear!
Let's start a campaign without more ado
495 And slay the Greeks and the Magyars, too.
A thousand men for you I'll lead.
The loss of my sons I rue indeed!"
   Then did the faithful Rother say:
"This I never can repay!
500 My father was wont to say to me
That whoever a worthy lord would be
Would be committing a grave mistake
If good advice he refused to take
Which was given to him for his own sake.
505 Now let us hasten to the court.
To all the nobles we should report
And also to each honest knight
(In this we shall only be doing right),
So that we may hear what they think of it
510 And derive from their counsel some benefit.
Supposing that there is some man
Who can work out a better plan
Than the one which we now entertain.
Ought we to set out for the Greek domain
515 Along with a mighty company
When we don't know for a certainty
Whether the envoys aren't still alive?
Perhaps grim Death could not contrive
To overcome the noblemen.
520 If we attack with an army then,
The Greeks will slay the worthy men.
Now by Almighty God on high,
Who fashioned me to live and die,
I swear that my sorrow for them is deep!"
525 The gentlemen both began to weep.
   To him replied the ancient duke:

"O King, though you weren't so astute,
With you I still would gladly fare:
In your distress I also share.
530　Now call together, sire, your men.
Gladly would I learn from them
What they think ought to be our plan
Of spying out the Grecian land.
(That, my lord, is but good sense.)
535　Now is my suffering most intense
On account of the handsome sons I reared
Who have so strangely disappeared.
For the sake of your honor I bade them fare.
Now, dear sir, you are aware
540　As well as I am, certainly,
In what condition they may be.
Ah, may Almighty God above,
In token of His lasting love,
Allow that day to come around
545　When I may see them safe and sound!"
　　Then to the court King Rother hied
(The ancient duke was at his side)
And summoned those he held most dear
To counsel him what course to steer.
550　When it was told to the company
That the king would fare across the sea,
Then up rose many a worthy knight
And spoke as truly as he might.
Thereby they sought to help their lord
555　That honor might be his reward.
At once they went to discuss this thing
Before the apartment of the king.
Then they decided to advise
The king to fare in splendid guise
560　As an exiled man across the main:
His honor he thus could best retain.
Now at the court was an ancient duke
Whom their advice did by no means suit.
He said that the trip were better not made.
565　Then Berchter came to his children's aid.
"How now, you coward!" he did say;
"How dare you counsel the king this way!"
With his fist he struck him such a blow
That from his neck the blood did flow,
570　And for three weeks he was so weak
That he could neither hear nor speak.

Then Berchter's men were heard to say
That he had behaved in a proper way:
What cause had the other to add to his woe?
575 After all, their lord had suffered so —
More than any other there —
That to do him an injury was not fair.
   The duke had got the worst of it;
With a mighty blow he had been hit.
580 To Rother then the nobles pressed
To tell him what they thought was best.
Among themselves they raised the question
Whether he would approve of their suggestion.
They said: "We've hit on a scheme for you
585 Which shouldn't be too hard to do.
We don't think it wise to make a campaign.
However, if you won't refrain,
No better way can you survive
Than by crossing the sea in an exile's guise.
590 For if the Greeks should be attacked,
This you know to be a fact:
Great harm to us will they contrive.
And should the envoys be still alive,
Then they will surely be ordered slain:
595 From this the Greeks will not refrain.
Now let it be your pleasure
To bring forth gold and treasure,
Of which you have a mighty hoard
Lying in your chamber stored.
600 You're rich enough in that, I think!
Share it wisely and do not stint,
And in this way, my noble lord,
Your honor will be soon restored.
Each of us has searched his mind,
605 And better counsel we cannot find.
If with us you do not agree,
You'll never come across the sea!"
   The mighty king replied to this
(Their counsel did not come amiss):
610 "You have not counseled badly.
I will obey you gladly.
You always shared in my distress.
Now this is the height of faithfulness,
That you do not abandon me
615 Now that I need you so urgently.
In truth, I have a mighty treasure.

Now may that man know God's displeasure
Who would stint with it in any way,
No matter whither he chance to stray."
620 Then he ordered four of his men to ride
Throughout the kingdom far and wide
And spread the news to young and old
That whoever wished to win much gold
Ought to set out upon the way
625 To the court at Rome without delay:
He needed their presence for a thing
Which to an end he could not bring
Without the help of many a knight
If it were to turn out for him all right.
630 Then he sent his letter, so we hear tell,
To a land where a curious folk did dwell.
A giant (Asprian was his name)
Who to the court no longer came,
Got so excited by the news
635 That not a minute did he lose:
He set out at once for Rother's land
Together with many a curious man.
A troop of giants he led along.
They carried clubs that were awfully long.
640   Rother's invitation,
Without exaggeration,
Was spread abroad on every side.
Then noblemen began to ride.
They dressed themselves in such array
645 That they set out splendidly on their way.
Because the summons was from the court,
They had no choice but to report.
And so a mighty host he won.
In close formation they did come
650 The time that princes seventy-two
Came to Rome for the rendezvous.
   Now a lad most curious to behold
Came striding along the dusty road.
He was too heavy for any steed.
655 A very strange lad he seemed indeed!
A club of steel he bore along;
It measured twenty-four cubits long.
Because of it everyone had to stare.
'Twas the giant Asprian coming there!
660   As soon as Berchter espied this folk,
This is the way the hero spoke:

"Proper fellows I do see,
Doughty warriors certainly.
A splendid troop is drawing near,
665 Well-equipped with battle-gear.
Welcome them, my gracious lord,
As with your honor it may accord.
Each one has such a mighty frame!
Wherever did a king obtain
670 So many undaunted fighting-men?
Just let somebody anger them!
If he should dodge their club by luck
And with their sword they catch him up,
His life will not be worth a rap —
675 He can be very sure of that!
Now lead, O Rother, if you please,
Twelve such warriors overseas
And not a man will ever dare
To lead his people against us there
680 Unless with his life he is ready to pay.
Although they live so far away,
They have shown up here at the court
Well-equipped for your support."
   In the dust the giants strode along.
685 Gleaming helmets they had on
And coats of mail that shone so bright,
Made to fit them exactly right.
Clubs of steel and swords they wore;
And very long whips they also bore:
690 There where the lash was wont to be
A chain of iron one could see,
In which was many a mighty knot.
The people had but a single thought
When they espied these curious men:
695 What might they now expect of them?
Fiercely they made ready to fight,
Clad in their corselets shining bright.
Truly, they were heroes keen!
When by Berchter this was seen,
700 Not a minute did he delay:
To them he quickly made his way.
Said he: "What's the reason for this to-do?
I forbid it to every one of you!"
The doughty lads made answer then:
705 "We do not trust those gentlemen!
We'll ward them off in such a way

That we may well survive this day!"
The duke replied: "They've come to the court
In order to lend us their support.
710 'Tis Asprian, a noble king,
Leading those giants along with him."
   Rother's behavior was most polite.
He greeted the giants all alike
As well as many a worthy man
715 Who had ridden thither to his land.
Then the excellent hero let them know
Just why he needed their presence so.
Said he: "Good warriors, hearken to me!
I must set sail across the sea
720 As though I'd been banished from my domain,
And shall adopt another name.
The Emperor Constantine has, I fear,
Struck off the heads of my envoys dear.
In truth, it is a year and a day
725 Since from our land they sailed away."
   As soon as they had been told this thing,
They hastened then to form a ring.
Truly, they were a mighty band!
At that time wisdom adorned each man.
730 And so they quickly decided then
That Berchter should rule over them
Until King Rother came back home,
For he could well defend the throne.
The noble duke replied thereto:
735 "I'm not the one to govern you.
If you entrust your lands to me,
Burned and plundered they will be,
Your borders violated,
Utterly devastated.
740 Choose for yourselves some other man!
In search of my sons I must leave the land.
Offer the crown to Amalger;
It will become him well, I swear!"
Then to Amalger they gave the throne
745 And the right to govern there at Rome.
This happened in a splendid ring.
(He was the lord of Tengeling.)
   Rother summoned to him then
Twelve dukes (they were comely men).

L. 747 *Tengeling* — in Upper Bavaria.

17

750 Behind each duke there marched along
Splendid knights two hundred strong,
Just as they had proudly come.
The excellent warriors every one
Stepped forth then to join the king
755 From the midst of the mighty gathering.
Behind King Asprian there went
A dozen of his regiment.
A giant was among them there
Of whom it was prudent to beware:
760 Just like a lion he went bound.
No fiercer fellow was ever found
Among the human race, I trow,
When from his chain he was let go.
If anybody got him mad,
765 His life wasn't worth a cent, begad!
He had made his way, so we hear tell,
From a country where the giants dwell
To put his valor to the test.
By threats and treatment of the best
770 He had been tamed by Asprian
So that he swore to be his man.
Widolt was the hero's name.
He was always in a savage frame.
    Rother bade his vassals true
775 Ride back home without ado
And help Sir Amalger guard the land
With all the means at their command
From evil men of every sort.
Quickly then he left the court
780 And came to Bari without delay,
Where there were waiting in the bay
The ships in which the noble king
Together with his following
Should venture forth across the sea.
785 The vessels were loaded speedily
With precious jewels and with gold,
With silks and satins fair to behold,
And with more wealth than one can say.
One came and carried it all away
790 From the chamber of the minghty king.
In wagons one made haste to bring
Inlaid work of every sort
To the vessels lying in the port.
    Then a man was led before the king

18

795 Who was able to fashion many a thing
　　So very skilfully out of gold
　　That it was a great pleasure to behold.
　　Words can't describe it in any way!
　　Never before the Judgment Day
800 Will there be found another man
　　To work such wonders with his hand.
　　　The ships were lying in the bay
　　All prepared to sail away.
　　Rother sent then for his harp
805 And bade his men and the giants embark.
　　At once they shoved off from the shore;
　　The rigging they began to draw.
　　They sailed to Constantinople Town,
　　The citadel of great renown,
810 Lying far across the main.
　　Then a clever thought to Rother came.
　　He said to his entire band:
　　"We're sailing to a foreign land.
　　Ours won't be an easy task, I fear.
815 Now this is what I want you to hear!
　　We all must be extremely sly
　　In case we do not want to die.
　　I wish to be called by everyone,
　　Both the old men and the young,
820 Dieterich in the days to come.
　　Thus no stranger will surmise
　　The nature of my enterprise."
　　Then all of them an oath did take,
　　Which no one later was to break,
825 To call him Dieterich as he bade.
　　He was heeded in this by many a lad.
　　　Splendidly the mighty band
　　Disembarked upon the strand.
　　The burghers then ran up to see
830 What wonderful items there might be:
　　The lovely wares they wished to behold.
　　All at once the giants bold
　　Started to fight upon the beach.
　　The townsfolk scattered out of reach.
835 Some of them were so distressed
　　That they outdistanced all the rest.
　　Then one of their number lost no time
　　In making his way to Constantine.
　　Said he: "O King, pray tell me true!

840 Whence comes this company to you?
They've journeyed here with so much might
That no one can describe it quite."
   Then to the man the queen did say:
"What can you tell us of their array?"
845 To this the burgher answered so:
"How am I supposed to know?
There were a great many of us folks
Who didn't get to inspect the boats.
Those terrible lads gave us such a scare
850 That we didn't do much looking there.
One of them lies bound to a chain,
Otherwise we'd have all been slain.
The only thing that occurs to me
About the things that one can see
855 Is that those lads have brought along
Iron clubs both big and long.
If there was anything more to see,
I cannot tell you what it might be."
   The giant fettered upon the strand
860 Received from them the strict command
To tarry there beside the sea
And keep watch over their property.
Then they dressed themselves in splendid wise:
They put on caps that drew all eyes.
865 They mounted mules as white as snow
(In Greece that was a very rare show).
They led by the hand along the way
Many a courser dapple-grey,
Handsome and of sturdy frame.
870 Wound about each horse's mane
Were pretty ribbons which had been lined
With precious stones of every kind.
Whithersoever the nobles rode,
The giants in their armor strode
875 Along the way as fast as they could.
   The Emperor was in a troubled mood.
He sat in council frequently
To find out who these lords might be.
One of his counselors then did say:
880 "Sire, you now will have to pay
For the way you treated those envoys fair
Whom you threw into your dungeon bare.
If these men should their masters be,
They will do to us an injury.

885 Some of us will be made to pay
Who never were guilty in any way.
Those fellows with the clubs, I swear,
Tower so high into the air
That no one can withstand them.
890 You've played the devil with your men!"
    Now it fell upon an Easter day
That Constantine with great array
Was holding court in the Hippodrome.
Many a lord stood near the throne.
895 Counts and dukes and barons fair —
All had been invited there
That they might add to his esteem.
From them the sweat began to stream:
That was on account of the fear they had
900 When the giants began to act like mad.
    When Dieterich and his following
Came into the presence of the king,
They got a courteous greeting then.
The dukes advanced to welcome them.
905 Likewise did the gracious queen:
She bowed to them with courteous mien
And bade that welcome they should be;
She greeted them decorously.
Then up to Asprian two counts went.
910 To take his club was their intent.
With so much steel had it been tipped,
They could not lift or carry it.
They had no choice but to drop it down
And leave it lying on the ground.
915   Constantine sat on his throne.
Dieterich drew near alone
And knelt politely in front of him.
He said: "I've long heard tell, O King,
About your magnanimity.
920 Now my distress, alas for me,
And my misfortune are so great,
It's beyond my power to relate.
Now honor God on me poor man,
For a king has put me in his ban.
925 Rother is the hero's name,
And he sits in the West beyond the main.
So great is the power he does wield
That everyone to him must yield.
When I was banished from his domain,

21

930 There no longer might I remain.
Then I knew that there was no place
Where I would ever be so safe
As here among your company —
So mighty are you said to be.
935 My homage I now offer you.
Accept it from me, hero true!
I've come here seeking your charity.
Now prove your honor, sire, on me!
If you refuse the service I tender,
940 My life to Rother I must surrender."
  All the while that Rother pled,
Asprian kept stamping his leg
Into the ground up to his thigh.
To Constantine there then drew nigh
945 The very wisest of his kin
Who at the court were serving him,
To counsel whether he could afford
To shelter there so many a lord.
Said he: "From Rother he's running away.
950 Here at my court he wants to stay.
He submits himself to me outright
And tells me of his grievous plight.
Now what shall we do with this exiled man?
I wish he had never come to our land!
955 And then to his men I must allude.
They seem to me extremely rude!
Their conduct is most indiscreet.
Just look at that fellow stamping his feet!
Such a lad in Hell should be
960 To keep the Devil company."
  The lords advised him to care for the men
So that they might be grateful to them.
"Of Rother it's little that we know;
These men could be a terrible foe.
965 To them we should so freely give
That they may be willing to let us live."
  To Dieterich he then did say
In a very overweening way:
"Some of my men have counseled me
970 To grant you hospitality.
If their advice had not been so,
How reluctantly I'd have let you go!
The stranger who at God's direction
Comes here in search of my protection

975 Can count upon it that he'll be served
Exactly as he has deserved.
But I don't esteem at all that man
Who journeys hither to my land
Only for the sake of gold.
980 Worthy man exceeding bold,
You come to us with a mighty crew;
They all pay fealty to you.
Acknowledge my authority
And the host here you yourself shall be,
985 Because it truly pleases me
That you seek my hospitality.
We thought that you had crossed the sea
To win the hand of a maiden fair
Whom I have reared with the greatest care.
990 I'd have done like Rother in that event
When he drove you into banishment.
I've got the better of him all the same!
The men who came here in his name
Are lying chained to my dungeon-floor.
995 Never will he see them more!
There were two men among them there
Such as an emperor might care
To count among his retinue.
They led here many a hero true."
1000   As soon as Asprian heard this speech,
For his shield he at once began to reach,
And demanded to have his battle-gear.
Said he: "Bad words one offers us here.
You do not give my lord his due;
1005 Rother sent good lads to you.
Whoever ordered them enchained,
For that may very well be blamed.
Now here in front of you we do stand.
Before your men can subdue our band,
1010 Laid out cold someone will be
(This I swear most solemnly!)
Who thought no one was as good as he —
If only my club doesn't break on me."
   Quickly he stepped into the ring.
1015 Then answered him the mighty king:
"Your anger causes me some surprise;
You've not been insulted in any wise.
That little speech which I just gave
Should not upset you, hero brave.

1020 My men have got me so drunk today
That like a fool I babble away.
That's why I shouldn't even try
To give a good lad a proper reply.
Now what I say, good sir, is true:
1025 I made that threat without meaning to,
For the wine in my head keeps going around,
And its effect is so profound
That over my tongue I have no command
When talking to your master's man."
1030   Asprian's anger passed away.
Then Dieterich's men did not delay:
They settled down so near the beach
That the vessels they could easily reach.
Quickly the stewards every one
1035 Who with Sir Dieterich had come
Procured twelve wagons all alike,
Which went full charged a sevennight.
They brought there all the treasure and gold
And whatever else the ships did hold —
1040 A very great hoard, so we hear tell.
Along went a man who guarded it well.
Six terrible giants kept driving him
And bade him raise up such a din
That all the people in the town
1045 Should never cease to spread around
Rumors about Sir Dieterich's crew.
Then he almost burst his chain in two.
He picked two rocks up from the ground
And with then he began to pound,
1050 So that great flames shot into the air.
Then the Greeks began to run from there.
Yet some chased after him all the time
Until he came before Constantine.
Then said a count for all to hear:
1055 "The Devil's bride is drawing near!
If only the shame which should be mine
Could ever be erased in time,
I swear by the Eternal Light
That I'd not wait here in the Emperor's sight!"
1060   As soon as the goodly queen espied
The lad who to a chain was tied,
She said: "Lord Constantine, I vow
That they're leading to you your master now,
Fastened to a chain, in troth!

1065 Alas! how stupid were we both
     To have kept our daughter from the man
     Who banished these fellows from his land.
     Such conduct wasn't very wise.
     May God Almighty now chastise
1070 Your peevish disposition!
     Ah, if my admonition
     You had, good sir, paid heed to then,
     You now could capture or slay these men.
     But I bet that whatever they ask of you,
1075 Out of fear you will agree to do
     And not at all because you're kind.
     If only they were of my mind,
     They'd bid you give the maid to them
     For whom you've slain so many men
1080 And brought so many into distress;
     Then I should see your cleverness!
     These lads don't seem to suit you right;
     They number so many a doughty knight.
     They are too strong for you, O King!
1085 Methinks you had rather dare to bring
     Your hand up sharp into your eye
     Than with his followers to vie
     Over even a tiny pin.
     Your conduct all this day has been
1090 Unworthy of a gentleman.
     Your drunkenness is but a sham!"
       The strangers stabled their steeds apace.
     In the courtyard then they took their place.
     They wrapped themselves in their mantles tight.
1095 Truly, their bearing was most polite
     As the noble Dieterich and his men
     Betook themselves to the palace then.
     They wore their swords into the hall.
     Among them was no place at all
1100 For the reproving courtier,
     Nor might he approach them anywhere,
     Because they fared with such array
     That never did the light of day
     Shine on Dieterich's like, I swear.
1105 The giant who lay fettered there
     Had clad himself in raiment fine.
     How the ruddy gold from him did shine!
     He wore a corselet made of gold;
     It signified their wealth untold.

1110 A helm of steel he also had
Which well became the honest lad.
Its border had with industry
Been ornamented skilfully
With many a jewel set in gold.
1115 Upon his legs the hero bold
Wore greaves of mail that were so fair
That they caught the eyes of the striplings there.
He also wore a surcoat fine.
Then said the men of Constantine:
1120 "Today we see the best dressed band
That ever journeyed to this land.
How wealthy must these warriors be,
While we live here so wretchedly!
That's because we serve a stingy lord
1125 Who thinks he never can afford
To make us any kind of pleasure —
So enamored is he of his treasure!"
    The draperies were hung anon.
Constantine came thereupon
1130 Into a splendid dining-hall.
Ah, what a press arose withal
When the noble Dieterich's following
Assembled there about the king!
They numbered many a goodly youth.
1135 A thousand doughty lads, in truth,
Had come with the exiled lord to dine
There in the palace of Constantine.
Then all the stewards hurried there
Who had the household in their care,
1140 And led Sir Dieterich to his seat
In a manner that was very meet.
Those in charge of the meat and wine
Had to remember all the time
To show great respect for Dieterich's men.
1145 They were very much afraid of them!
    Then one led a fierce lion before the king.
It had to be first in everything.
From the lads it took their bread away
And set the whole table in great dismay.
1150 With one hand Asprian grasped it
And against the wall he smashed it,
So that it was shattered all to bits.
How grieved was Constantine by this!
Yet he did not dare to blink an eye.

1155 Then said two dukes who were standing nigh:
"God alone is our resort
Against these gentlemen here at court!"
One of them departed then
And spoke thus to the serving-men:
1160 "A devilish fellow is in the hall!
He hurled the lion against the wall
Because it wanted to take his bread.
Carefully you had better tread!
If you will follow what I say,
1165 You'll keep out of that fellow's way
And allow him quietly to do
Whatever he has a liking to.
Unless you want to be done in,
Don't ever take his bread from him —
1170 Else with his hand he'll grasp you
And against the wall he'll smash you!"
    The queen had noticed without distress
The anger over the lion's death.
She laughed aloud at Constantine.
1175 "Now see", said she, "how that courtier fine
Standing before the table there
Has given your pet the best of care.
This is something I shan't forget!
Verily, you must now regret
1180 That you kept our daughter from the man
Who drove these fellows from his land.
If my advice you now would heed,
Then you would have the envoys freed
And sent back to their homes again;
1185 And you would give to each of them
Raiment of such quality
As one might offer honorably.
What better use for it could you find?
Consider, Constantine, in your mind!
1190 If these men couldn't put up a fight,
How could you oppose King Rother's might?
If he should inquire about his men,
Your land will suffer grievously then.
Now why don't you give the men to me
1195 Who are languishing here so miserably,
That I may bring them into the air.
How very wretchedly they fare!"
    Then he said that this he would never do,
Even though one tried to force him to.

1200 It was no use for her to ask:
They still would have to feel his wrath,
Whether or not it gave her pain.
On the soil of Greece they must remain
As long as he still had his life.
1205 Then said again the queen his wife:
"What miracles would you perform on them?
After all, they're only men!
They come from Adam like everyone.
To God let honor now be done
1210 And let the wretched men go free.
Give them back their liberty!
Of health they have been cheated;
Cruelly they've been treated.
Alas for their fair manhood!
1215 If only I poor woman could
Obtain the help of such a man
To work against the Emperor's plan
As that brave fellow fettered there,
Back to their homeland they would fare.
1220 No matter how much you counsel me,
... ...
Ere it should cause you any pain,
How willingly would he refrain."
 Berchter said to his master then:
"In the queen we seem to have found a friend.
1225 It may not have injured us at all
That the lion was smashed against the wall:
It seems to have made her very glad.
But none of the others would be sad
If we were to go so far away
1230 That they need see us from this day
Here in their country nevermore.
So many men walk through the door
Muttering beneath their breaths
That I doubt whether we are welcome guests.
1235 They're none of them sure they'll survive this day.
Put their minds at rest, I pray!
Free them of their great concern
And to our lodging let's return,
So that those exiled to this ground,
1240 Of whom so many are walking around

L. 1220 Some lines seem to have been omitted here.

       Suffering most grievously
       (How poverty-stricken they must be!),
       Can share in your inheritance.
       May God of His benevolence
1245   Allow them to forget their pain.
       Surely in their own domain
       They all were lords of high esteem.
       Here the life they live is mean.
       The pity I feel for them is great.
1250   Help them for your honor's sake!
       You are richer than Constantine.
       Why at his table should you dine?
       It doesn't become us at all, you know."
       Then Dieterich made answer so:
1255   "You are, I swear, a vassal true —
       For which may God be good to you!
       If from your counsel I turn away,
       No other man will I obey."
          As soon as they began to dine,
1260   Dieterich went to Constantine
       And said: "'Twould please me well, O sire,
       If to my lodging I might retire
       So that with my followers I might be.
       They weren't all able to come with me.
1265   Whenever to the court I fare,
       Many a man must tarry there
       Where we all have our lodging-place.
       My lady, show us now your grace,
       Because I lead a wretched band:
1270   My best men I no longer command.
       Those who paid honor to my name
       Have by King Rother all been slain.
       There in his realm I might not bide."
          To him King Constantine replied:
1275   "Reluctantly we grant your plea.
       Repair now to your hostelry.
       If aught of mine finds favor with you,
       It shall be yours without ado.
       I wish to take you into my pay
1280   And honor you in every way
       So that the more willing your man may be
       To behave at table courteously,
       Because he terrifies my wife
       Who is as dear to me as my life.
1285   My men aren't bothered by it at all;

They've often recovered from such a brawl.
But here in this hall it's rarely been tried."
The giant Asprian then replied:
"In truth, sire, I was sore bestead.
1290 Your bear-cub took away my bread."
    The noble Dieterich went apace
To where they had their lodging-place,
And acted for a fortnight
As if he were an errant knight,
1295 Until Almighty God began
To send to him many an exiled man.
To them the gates were never closed;
They went out and in just as they chose.
Dieterich cared for their needs himself
1300 And gladly shared with them his wealth.
Berchter and Asprian did the same,
And so did the others in Dieterich's train:
They greeted them in courteous fashion
And on their misery took compassion.
1305 For them the table was often spread.
Whoever wanted to be fed
Was sure of getting a meal there.
And so to the hero they did repair.
One treated them with the utmost tact
1310 And gave them whatsoever they lacked —
Of which the poor men stood in need,
For till then no one had paid them heed.
From all parts of the city then
Dieterich got a host of men
1315 Who had put up with great distress
In order to prove their fearlessness.
Because they had neither horses nor gear,
At Constantine's court they might not appear.
And so those men of high degree
1320 Had to live most wretchedly.
    Soon the exiles understood
That they were well liked by the hero good
Who now belonged to Constantine's court.
And so to Dieterich did report
1325 A mighty host of fighting-men.
How generously he gave to them!
He treated them like his own kin.
He seated them right next to him.
He gave his butlers all a sign
1330 To keep their goblets filled with wine;

     And all his stewards he directed
     That they should in no wise be neglected.
     And so in front of every guest
     Nourishment of the very best
1335 Which could be gotten anywhere
     Was placed on the table for their fare.
        As soon as the gentlemen had dined
     And had put some of their cares behind,
     Then all who were of knightly estate
1340 Were bidden to go from the others straight.
     One gave them horses of noble breed
     And silken cloaks that were fair indeed,
     And along with the horses coats of mail,
     So that no sword might make them quail.
1345 Then Asprian came hurrying there
     With many a mantle passing fair
     From the noble Dieterich's chamber
     And arrayed alike each stranger.
     He gave a sword to every man
1350 And put a pennon in his hand.
     Then on their steeds they began to joust
     And rejoiced aloud at every thrust.
     Because of this Sir Dieterich's praise
     Was heard at the court for many days.
1355   Then there came a troop of warriors fair
     Who had been delayed in getting there.
     Because it was so late in the day,
     They feared that they'd be turned away.
     Berchter walked about the men,
1360 Seeking to discern on them
     What sort of figure each one had.
     He saw there many a naked lad
     Seated before him deeply shamed.
     To Dieterich Berchter then exclaimed:
1365 "Cast your eyes on these wretched men!
     May God be merciful unto them!
     How sorely are they mortified
     Because their shame they cannot hide!
     To all of them you should donate
1370 Clothes befitting their estate.
     They are so narrow in the waist,
     Their bearing is so full of grace
     That they can have no other thought
     But to behave as good knights ought.
1375 Truly, the glances of their eyes

They cast in such decorous wise
That men like these could never be
Other than of high degree.
I allow you to strike off my head
1380　If some of them aren't nobly bred!"
"Your counsel," said Dieterich, "pleases me.
Whoever seeks my charity
Shall find it if it please the Lord."
Then of his goods a mighty hoard
1385　Was set before the strangers there.
In the name of Christ each took his share.
　　Now it wasn't very long, we're told,
Ere Dieterich, the hero bold,
Had gained for himself six thousand men,
1390　Who were very glad to promise then
That they would serve him every day.
They suited a lord in every way.
　　To Constantinople there came a man
Whom war had driven from his land.
1395　Arnold was the good count's name,
And he had three barons in his train.
They found themselves in the direst straits
Because they had given up great estates
When they had fled their native ground.
1400　There in the town they walked around
Naked and lamenting sore,
Since no one would open to them his door.
A merchant then drew near their side
(No better was there far and wide)
1405　And said: "My lords, it's plain to see
That you aren't used to poverty.
If you will now agree to do
Exactly as I counsel you,
To Dieterich you will repair.
1410　He will take care of you, I swear,
So that you'll forget your wretched state.
And if aught from me you deign to take,
Then I will equip you with such gear
That henceforth you won't need to fear
1415　Lest anybody see your shame."
"May God reward you for the same,"
The worthy Arnold said thereto;
"And this I solemnly swear to you,
That if the lord be good to me,
1420　I shall repay your charity."

The exiled count did not delay:
At once he set out on his way
To Dieterich's lodging with his kin.
Politely Dieterich greeted him
1425 And showed him every courtesy.
Then he inquired who he might be.
Mournfully the count replied:
"My enemies have in their pride
Banished me from my own land.
1430 Before you stands a needy man.
And yet however poor I be,
My lineage does make me free.
I have betaken myself to you
In search of your mercy, hero true."
1435 Said Dieterich: "Be of good cheer!"
From Berchter then he wished to hear
What presents they could give the lord
Which with his honor might accord.
The ancient man replied thereto:
1440 "God has been generous to you:
He bestowed on you great wealth indeed.
Now help this gentleman in his need.
And if you hold my counsel dear,
Then let the treasure be carried here.
1445 Stinginess was never our sin.
Give a thousand pounds to him
And add a little more to it.
And I shall also do my bit
To help him get the best estate
1450 That in this town we can locate."
"Upon my word," said Asprian,
"I also want to help the man.
I promise to provide the gear
For thirty warriors every year."
1455   Dieterich liked the advice he had got.
He had the famous treasure brought
And gave the noble count a share.
Joyfully did the latter fare
To Constantine without more ado
1460 And said to him and his retinue:
"Dieterich gave this to me.
God grant that prosperous he may be!"
To this remarked the gentle queen:
"He is of noble birth, I ween.
1465 Now judge how clever is Constantine.

33

What suffering must now be mine,
Seeing my daughter might not wed
The man from whom this hero fled.
If the latter behaves so worthily,
1470 How noble then must Rother be!
He surely is a mighty king."
Then said the Emperor's following:
"Lady, how true is what you've said!
Now may the Devil strike them dead
1475 Who were in any way to blame
That here in this land we did remain
And never joined up with Rother's men.
He would have sent us home again
Rich in honors of every kind.
1480 Now each of us has set his mind —
Since that, alas, can never be —
On swearing to Dieterich fealty.
With us he'll share his treasure
And enrich us beyond measure."
1485   The exiled count then did not stay:
He repaired to Dieterich straight away
Together with his kinsmen three.
He greeted them decorously
And sent them on into the town.
1490 A palace for them Berchter found,
And Asprian provided there
Thirty warriors passing fair
And furnishings of every sort.
Then all the nobles at the court
1495 Made up their minds up that, come what may,
Nothing was going to stand in their way
Of swearing to be Sir Dieterich's men.
To him the barons hastened then
Along with the counts of high degree
1500 And all the rest of the company
Who served at the court of Constantine.
Only the great dukes stayed behind.
(Of that our story speaks them free —
And they didn't do it, verily!)
1505 But the other brave lads went apace
To the noble Dieterich's lodging-place:
They proceeded there with great array.
He bestowed upon them every day
Not only plenty of ruddy gold
1510 And uncut bolts of silk, we're told,

But also mantles white as snow —
For which they were not loath to go.
One saw the giant Asprian then
Run to the storeroom and back again
1515 Many a time until each wish
Had been fulfilled by Dieterich.
Then all the nobles with one accord
Began to praise the noble lord.
There wasn't a single man, I swear,
1520 Who had accepted his bounty there
But wished to remain in his command
At the risk of banishment from the land.
    As soon as the knights had returned to court
With handsome gifts of every sort,
1525 Then many a demoiselle began
Whispering behind her hand
In the princess' chamber
About the noble stranger
At all hours of the day and night —
1530 How splendidly behaved the knight!
Then said the princess: "Advise me how
I can persuade my father now
To let us see the noble lord
So that with decorum it may accord."
1535 Said Herlint: "I don't rightly know.
You are his only child, and so
You are to him extremely dear.
Get him to give a party here
To which shall come the hero true.
1540 Upon my word I swear to you
That there's no better way to see the man.
We shall never hit on a better plan!"
    Thereupon the damsel went
To Constantine's apartment
1545 And said: "If you, my father dear,
This Easter should be staying here,
It would seem to me a fitting thing
To invite to the court your following,
So that the heroes may proclaim
1550 How richly you deserve your fame.
I don't know what good a prince may be
If at his court occasionally
There isn't rejoicing on every side."
To this the Emperor replied:
1555 "Blessings on you, daughter mine!

How towards honor you incline!
As always your counsel is the best.
Now I shall ask so many a guest
That one will always want to hear
1560 About the revelry and the cheer
At Constantine's festivity.
So great is the power invested in me
That if somebody stays away,
With his life he will be made to pay."
1565 Back to her chamber the maiden went.
Then Constantine the Mighty sent
Messengers throughout the land
And ordered many a nobleman
To come there to his celebration.
1570 They all accepted his invitation.
Safe-conduct they were guaranteed,
So they had no choice but to proceed.
If anyone was reluctant to,
One threatened to hang him without ado.
1575 And so they preferred to make the trip
Rather than hang on account of it:
They had no choice but to consent.
Straightway every noble went
And sought the company of his peer.
1580 Carefully they prepared their gear.
Not a mantle could one behold
Which wasn't trimmed with cloth of gold.
And such things were so plentiful there
That at them no one thought to stare.
1585 The mightiest princes of the land
Came together in a band
And journeyed to the Hippodrome.
Then sixteen dukes set out from home
With thirty counts coming close behind.
1590 In the city then they all reclined
And shared the wealth of Constantine.
(This custom still holds in our own time.)
 When they came to Constantinople Town,
The citadel of great renown,
1595 The princes lodged there overnight
In a style that suited them just right.
As soon as the day began to break,
Each steward went to the hall to take
On behalf of his lord that place therein
1600 Which the court had seen fit to assign to him.

　　　　Then Asprian set out forthwith
　　　　To occupy for Dieterich
　　　　The place of honor, so we're told.
　　　　Eagerly then the giant bold
1605　　Set up a very splendid chair
　　　　Which had, in truth, been carried there
　　　　Heretofore from Ireland.
　　　　As far as I can understand,
　　　　Of ivory it had been made,
1610　　And with rare stones it was inlaid.
　　　　However dark the night might be,
　　　　The jewels shone forth radiantly.
　　　　Then Asprian prepared a board
　　　　In such a way that his mighty lord
1615　　Might there with honor take his seat.
　　　　Now a proud lord was in the Emperor's suite,
　　　　A duke named Friederich, I declare,
　　　　Whose steward was late in getting there.
　　　　To Asprian the latter cried
1620　　That he should move his chairs aside;
　　　　And he told the giant in addition
　　　　How lofty was his lord's position:
　　　　He claimed for him as noble a line
　　　　As that of the Emperor Constantine.
1625　　Said he: "Make room, you ugly ape!
　　　　The place of honor is ours to take."
　　　　"Upon my word," sir Asprian said,
　　　　"You'd better put that out of your head.
　　　　The court assigned this place to me.
1630　　You've no right here, that's plain to see.
　　　　If you are thinking of acting tough,
　　　　You'll soon wish you were smart enough
　　　　To have put it off for another day
　　　　When it would not cause such dismay —
1635　　That would seem to me a better plan!
　　　　Now go pick on some other man
　　　　And leave my chairs right where they stand."
　　　　　The haughty steward of the duke
　　　　Was greatly irked by this rebuke.
1640　　He had with him a hundred men
　　　　On whom he believed he could depend.
　　　　And so he thought that Asprian,
　　　　By disobeying his command,
　　　　Had shown how foolish one could get.
1645　　One of his benches he upset.

Asprian, the hero true,
Raised his hand without more ado
And gave the fellow a slap so smart
That at once his skull was split apart.
1650 Then for their shields his followers ran:
They wanted to do in Asprian.
Duke Friederich did not delay:
He donned his armor straight away
And called on his friends to help him out.
1655 Then there arose a mighty shout
That the noble Dieterich's seneschal
Was being attacked within the hall
By a mighty company of thanes.
The giant who was bound by chains
1660 Began to roar just like a bear
And broke the chains he was forced to wear.
He took a steel club in his hand
(Four-and-twenty ells it spanned).
Whoever happened to cross his path
1665 Had little chance to survive his wrath.
Then a giant named Grimme began to call:
"Things look pretty bad inside the hall!
I notice Widolt on the move.
Now, Sir Asprian, you can prove
1670 Whether you're truly a worthy man."
Cleverly then Sir Asprian
Began to ask the giant grim
What injury had been done to him
To make him behave so savagely.
1675 "My lord, it had been told to me,"
The valiant Widolt then replied,
"That you were beset on every side.
Since I didn't know who was to blame,
I wanted to see the whole lot slain.
1680 If anyone has made you wroth,
He must surrender his life, in troth!"
"Verily," said Asprian then,
"Nothing have I had from them
But what is honorable and good.
1685 Give over now this angry mood!
Yield your club to yonder man."
Then a giant took it from his hand.
  The haughty duke was filled with pain
When he learned that his steward had been slain.
1690 Then all the members of his band

      Hurried there with sword in hand
      And wanted to do Sir Asprian in.
      Then Widolt wanted to hear from him
      Who were those fellows drawing near.
1695 "Ah, if only my club were here!
      To harm you, master, is their wish.
      Today they'll dearly pay for this!
      If I don't happen first to die,
      Reason enough they'll have to cry.
1700 Now watch how I make them all retreat!"
      With his fist he knocked one off his feet
      And got the good duke in his grasp,
      And tore away his steel casque.
      Then by his hair he lifted him high,
1705 And into the crowd he let him fly.
      Wherever he seized the other men,
      It began to sprout like chickweed then.
      Many a lad got such a thump
      That he came back to earth with a mighty bump.
1710 Now I don't know how a gleeman came
      Running to the court amain
      And told the king that a terrible brawl
      Had broken out within the hall.
         Constantine inquired of him
1715 What the reason was for all the din.
      "By the holy Christ," he made reply,
      "I'll tell you how the ground does lie.
      Some fellow there kept dishing out grub
      With what must be the longest club
1720 That ever was seen in any land,
      Until they forced it from his hand.
      To all of them he shows respect:
      Not a single one does he neglect.
      Whomever he grabs hold of there
1725 He yanks most awfully by the hair.
      How lucky was I to escape so soon!
      Over four fellows he let me zoom
      So that I sailed right through the air
      And never touched earth anywhere.
1730 I was only blocking his light, you see.
      He didn't have any use for me."
         Widolt was restrained once more,
      Bound to the chain as heretofore.
      As soon as he was led away,
1735 Then everyone without delay

Ran to the Emperor with his tale.
Bitterly they all did wail
Because Sir Dieterich's seneschal
Had roughed them up within the hall.
1740 Said Constantine: "I am aghast!
Now tell his master what has passed.
I'd like him to make it up to you.
But with this affair I'll have nothing to do."
As soon as Dieterich heard the news,
1745 Then not a minute did he lose.
He sent his men to his lodging-place
To bring the giant to court apace.
"If he has harmed you in any way,
With his life he shall be made to pay
1750 Here in the presence of all of you."
"This matter we'd rather not pursue,"
The proud Duke Friederich made reply,
"Than that the devil to court should hie
Where we would have to see his face
1755 If he were to show up in this place."
Then they took each other by the hand
And before the king they went to stand.
They said: "O Dieterich, we implore you!
Don't summon that fellow here before you!
1760 He hasn't caused us so much pain
That any of us would ever complain.
Inasmuch as you've fled here from your foes,
You should be honored, Jesus knows!
By everyone in this domain,
1765 Else all of us must suffer shame."
Then Dieterich thanked the gentlemen.
Sore afraid were some of them
That many a blow on them would fall
To make them forget about the brawl
1770 If the giant showed up a second time
There at the court of Constantine.
And so they never did complain.
They all concealed their disgrace and shame.
The men who had been tousled there
1775 Kept silent about the whole affair,
Even though it pleased them not.
Constantine sat deep in thought
And complained about it to the queen.
"Alas, how shamed I now have been
1780 That such a thing was ever done

To guests who to my court did come
From many a land at my invitation.
They've suffered such humiliation —
Pulled by the hair and knocked about —
1785 That their lamenting may never die out.
It was Dieterich's man who began it, too,
Just on account of a chair or two!
His onslaught no one could resist.
He knocked them all down with his fist
1790 So that in the mud they came to lie.
For the archers they should have raised a cry.
Then he might easily have been hit
So that he'd have had no joy of it —
For which I'd always have been glad!"
1795 "Be silent now," the good queen bade,
"And let us not pursue this matter.
You know it's only idle chatter.
If he had stood so near to you
That you could have seen all you wanted to,
1800 No good at all would a bow have been:
You would have run away from him
Ahead of the others, I declare!
But if you had given our daughter fair
To the mighty king beyond the main,
1805 No one would dare to cause you shame.
From his domain he would have sent
Warriors so excellent
That no one could invade your land
Even with a mighty band.
1810 Reason enough have I to complain!
Suffer now the disgrace and shame
Here in your realm as best you can
At the hands of the noble Dieterich's man."
    The Emperor let the matter drop
1815 And sent for his daughter on the spot.
He bade the maiden take her way
To the dining-hall without delay.
Most willingly did she consent:
To visit the court was her intent.
1820 And so without any hesitating
She set out with her maids-in-waiting —
A hundred damsels passing fair,
All with flaxen-colored hair.
Many a bracelet could one behold,
1825 Fashioned out of the ruddy gold.

Now our story will digress
To tell you something about their dress.
The maiden who led all the rest
Had made herself the prettiest.
1830 She wore a crown of gold so fine
(It was at the bidding of Constantine).
The other maidens one and all
Wore splendid raiment to the hall
In token of their high esteem.
1835 Silken stuffs of splendid sheen
Had been embroidered, so we're told,
Through and through with thread of gold
And lined with sable and with vair.
Many a gentleman had to stare
1840 When he beheld the damsel fair
Leading her maids-in-waiting there.
　Then a band of noblemen made their way
Into the hall without delay.
Dieterich was in the van;
1845 He led there many a doughty man.
So marvelous was their array
That never before or since that day
Was raiment seen that could compare
With what the heroes were wearing there.
1850 Their shirts were woven of silk, we're told;
Their caps were made of cloth of gold
And adorned with many a precious stone.
From Dieterich a ruby shone.
It was a jewel so passing fine
1855 That many another it did outshine
Which would have got the highest praise
If it had not drawn everyone's gaze.
　How in the world could mantles be
Fashioned more becomingly
1860 To enhance a hero's bearing
Than what those knights were wearing?
Lined with ermine was every fold
And covered over with cloth of gold.
If anyone was standing near,
1865 Green as grass it did appear.
As soon as the color no longer shone,
The fairest jewel to look upon
Gleamed in all its nobility.
What thing more precious could there be?
1870 Besides all this, it smelled sweet.

A people called the Flatfeet
Had honored Asprian therewith.
Later he gave it to Dieterich.
That was the reason why Dieterich's cloak
1875 Was so admired by all the folk
Who had assembled on the spot.
Because they stood around and gawked,
The damsel was cheated of her delight:
She never got to see the knight.
1880   The festival continued on
Until three days had come and gone.
On the morning of the final day
The wandering minstrels made their way
To where Sir Dieterich's table stood.
1885 Christ knows, he gave as a gentleman should!
The worthy lord could not say no.
His handsome cloak he did bestow
Upon a minstrel worn with care
Who was lucky enough to have hurried there.
1890 The others followed his example:
Not a knight retained his mantle
Of those whom Dieterich had brought.
In very truth, it mattered not
To whom they gave their cloaks away.
1895 Not one did they keep for themselves that day!
   The festival had reached an end.
All the guests began to wend
Back to their homelands once again,
With the exception of Dieterich's men.
1900 To their abode they all withdrew
And dressed themselves in garments new.
... ...
He proved himself so excellent there
That never before or since, I swear,
Lived there a hero anywhere
1905 Who was the noble Dieterich's peer.
And so we gladly praise him here
Because of the excellence he did show.
With everyone it wasn't so.
   The festival had come and gone.
1910 Then everyone repaired anon
To the chamber of the youthful queen

  L. 1901. A line is missing here.

To tell about the clothes they'd seen.
Truly, they were much impressed
With the way that Dieterich had been dressed.
1915 As soon as one went through the door,
Another stationed himself before
Until the maiden had heard so much
That in her heart she felt the touch
Of tender passion for the man
1920 Who had journeyed thither to her land.
At that time she still was a stranger to him.
With the hero later she was to win
Her share of this world's gladness,
Together with some sadness.
1925   Within the chamber quiet reigned.
The lovely princess then complained:
"Ah, Dame Herlint, now you see
How my thoughts must always be
With the noble Dieterich.
1930 It is, in truth, my fondest wish
That I might see him secretly —
If that could be done with propriety
On the part of the very worthy knight.
With five of my bracelets I would requite
1935 The one who should not hesitate
To take a message from me straight
And swiftly bring the stranger
Hither to my chamber."
Said Herlint: "I'm the one to send!
1940 Upon your errand I shall wend,
Whether or not it bring us shame:
To the hero's lodging I'll go amain.
For virtue he's so famous
That he will never shame us."
1945   The lady Herlint did not stay:
She went to a chamber straight away
And chose for herself a splendid dress
Such as ladies oft possess.
As soon as she had put it on,
1950 The clever maid set out anon
To the noble Dieterich's residence.
He welcomed her there with deference.
Beside him then she took a seat
And into his ear began to speak:
1955 "My mistress bids me say to you
That she offers her devotion true:

44

Her love for you she does avow.
Go to her apartment now.
Waiting there the maid will be
1960 To greet you with such courtesy
As with your honor may well accord.
You can be sure of this, my lord,
That in my mistress you will find
Devotion of the truest kind."
1965   Now hear the answer that Dieterich gave!
"You're guilty, ma'am, of a sin most grave
By treating thus a stranger.
To many a lady's chamber
I've gone before when that might be.
1970 Now why do you make fun of me?
The poor have always been treated so.
Those aren't your lady's words, I trow!
So many dukes and princes, too,
Are in the Emperor's retinue
1975 That you might just as well have had
Your little joke with another lad —
Less blame would you have earned thereby!
In Hell you now deserve to fry
For wanting to make a fool of me.
1980 Howsoever poor I be,
I once was held in high esteem
As a mighty count in my demesne!"
   Then said Dame Herlint to the knight
(She knew how to choose her words aright):
1985 "O no, Sir Dieterich, I implore you —
Don't think that's why I've come before you!
God knows, whatever I said is true!
My mistress bade me come to you.
In very truth, she is amazed
1990 That you've been at the court these many days
And have not asked in all this time
To see the daughter of Constantine.
Seldom has a splendid knight
Committed such an oversight.
1995 Now don't reprove me for my speech.
Whatever heights you yet may reach,
'Twill please the princess well, I vow,
Though you do not care to see her now.
But if you were to visit her,
2000 'Twould not turn out amiss, dear sir."
   Now listen to the lord's reply

(He knew that the lady did not lie):
"There are so many informers here
That the man who holds his honor dear
2005 Must conduct himself with the greatest care.
The homeless man is well aware
That he can never behave so well
That all who at the court do dwell
Will look upon him favorably.
2010 Now tell your mistress this for me:
My service I do offer her;
But any visit I must defer
Lest it should be misunderstood.
I sorely fear that we both could
2015 Be slandered very grievously.
Then Constantine would banish me
Forevermore from his domain.
Then I should have to flee, good dame,
From Rother as long as I drew breath
2020 And nowhere should be safe from Death."
 Herlint wished to be on her way.
The noble Dieterich bade her stay
And summoned his goldsmiths there to him.
He bade them speedily begin
2025 To cast a pair of silver shoes
(Not a minute did they lose)
And a pair of golden shoes as well,
Such as might suit a demoiselle;
And he bade Sir Asprian see to it
2030 That on one foot alone should fit
The pair of shoes which he then should take
And give to the lady Herlint straight
Along with a mantle fair to behold
And a dozen rings of ruddy gold.
2035 (That is the proper way, I ween,
To thank the confidante of a queen!)
Then over the yard she skipped with pleasure
Back to her mistress with her treasure.
 Herlint did not hesitate:
2040 To the princess' chamber she hurried straight
And told her how, in very truth,
Dieterich, the noble youth,
Was much concerned for his good name.
"This is what I learned, good dame:
2045 He holds the Emperor's favor dear.
He says that he may not see you here,

Else his good name he'd surely lose.
Now cast your eyes on these lovely shoes!
They were given to me by the worthy knight
2050 With other things of much delight.
Upon my word, this mantle fair
(Lucky me that I went there!)
And these twelve armlets fair to see
The excellent man bestowed on me.
2055 Never could there be, I swear,
A knight more winsome anywhere
Upon this earth than Dieterich.
May God not strike me dead for it,
But I stared at him against my will —
2060 On account of which I am blushing still."
 The princess answered: "Now I see
That happiness is not for me,
Since to visit me he doesn't choose.
If you will give me now these shoes,
2065 You can have all the gold that goes therein:
That's because of my regard for him."
At once the exchange was agreed upon.
The golden shoe she first drew on,
And then the silver one she took.
2070 It would only go on the selfsame foot!
"Oh goodness me!" the maid exclaimed.
"How both of us have now been shamed!
Whoever selected these shoes so fair
Has made an error, I declare.
2075 I never shall get this one on!
In truth, you must again be gone
And ask Sir Dieterich for me
(Display the utmost courtesy!)
To let you have the other shoe
2080 And visit me here without more ado,
Provided he should really be
A man of true gentility."
 "Oh dear!" Dame Herlint then replied,
"How sorely are we mortified
2085 Because of this, my mistress dear!
Now this I can tell you without fear,
That though the shame be always mine,
I'm ready to go there another time."
The lovely maiden thereupon
2090 Lifted the dress which she had on
All the way up to her knee.

Not a thought did she give to propriety!
She quite forgot a lady's gait.
Across the yard she hurried straight
2095 To the noble Dieterich's residence.
He greeted her with deference
And put on a demeanor
As if he had never seen her.
And yet he was at once aware
2100 Why she again had hurried there.
    To Dieterich said the damsel then:
"It is my duty once again
To bring a message to you here.
A mistake was made with the shoes, I fear.
2105 I gave them to my dame, that's true,
But only out of regard for you.
Now we would like the proper one.
My lady bade that I should come
And ask that you give to her the mate
2110 And request that you come and see her straight,
In case you really claim to be
A man of true gentility."
    Said he: "I'd go there willingly,
But the chamberlains would peach on me."
2115 Said Herlint: "They are not at home;
They're watching the games at the Hippodrome.
The knights are hurling the javelin;
In games of war they seek to win.
Now I will go ahead of you.
2120 Of your retainers take but two
And follow after me, I pray,
To my lady's chamber without delay.
No one will see you passing by
On account of all the hue and cry.
2125 I shall see to it, hero fair,
That the princess alone will be waiting there."
    Herlint wished to be on her way.
The clever fellow then did say:
"Wait till I question my chamberlain.
2130 I'll find out about the shoes from him."
Swiftly Asprian showed his head.
"Ah, what did I do to you?" he said.
"All these tasks I can't complete!
You've kept me the whole day on my feet
2135 With always some new job to do,
More than you ever did hitherto!

         A great many shoes were cast today
         Which the lads have carried all away.
         If any of them we still can get,
2140   You soon shall have them to inspect."
         Thereupon the giant took
         The lovely shoes for the other foot
         And a mantle very fair to behold
         And a dozen rings of ruddy gold,
2145   And gave it all to the lady fair.
         Stealthily she went from there
         In a most contented frame of mind
         And left Sir Dieterich behind.
         To her mistress then she hastened to tell
2150   A piece of news which pleased her well.
            Impatiently the damsels waited.
         Dieterich deliberated
         How he might see the maiden fair
         Without any scandal whatsoe'er.
2155   "That's easily done," said Berchter then.
         "At the Hippodrome I'll have my men
         Raise up such a hue and cry
         That everyone will hurry by
         And no one will pay you any heed."
2160   Then he ordered the giants to proceed,
         And saddled himself his courser fair.
         Quickly they set out from there.
         The old boy galloped at their head;
         A thousand men-at-arms he led.
2165   Widolt with the club, we're told,
         Hurried then along the road,
         Jumping up and down like mad
         Just as if he were a stag.
         Asprian came tumbling along
2170   (He was the minstrel of the throng).
         Twelve full fathoms Grimme sprang,
         And so did the others of his band.
         Then he seized a rock of monstrous size.
         The result was that none of the spies
2175   Noticed Dieterich for the shouting
         When the giants set out on their outing.
            Before the window stood the dame.
         Hurrying over the courtyard came
         Dieterich, the youthful knight.
2180   The greeting he got was most polite.
         Accompanied by heroes twain,

Dieterich to the maiden came.
Quickly the door was opened wide.
The handsome fellow stepped inside.
2185 To meet him went the youthful queen
And welcomed him with courteous mien.
She said that whatever his wish might be
She would fulfill it willingly,
If with their honor it might accord.
2190 "I wished to speak with you, my lord,
Because you are said to have no peer:
That is the reason I asked you here.
Concerning this pair of shoes so neat —
Help me to draw them on my feet!"
2195 "With pleasure", Dieterich replied.
"To you can nothing be denied."
The hero knelt then at her feet
In a manner that was very meet.
She put her foot upon his lap.
2200 No lady was better shod than that!
The clever fellow then did say:
"Madam, hear my words, I pray!
Tell me in all honesty,
As a Christian you would be:
2205 Since you've been wooed by so many men,
If you could choose from all of them,
Who is the man from all that host
That pleases you the very most?"
   To him the damsel said: "I vow
2210 To answer your question truthfully now.
Sir, by my immortal life,
As I would be a Christian wife,
If in response to some command
The bravest heroes from every land
2215 Were to assemble on common ground,
Never would a man be found
Who might claim to be your equal there.
By all that I hold dear I swear
That never did a woman bear
2220 A child so comely anywhere
That with propriety it might
Sit beside you, worthy knight,
So excellent have you proved to be.
But if the choice were up to me,
2225 I'd take a bold and worthy man
Whose envoys journeyed to this land

And since have spent a weary time
In the dungeon of Lord Constantine.
Rother is that hero's name,
2230 And he dwells in the West beyond the main.
A maiden I shall always be
Unless the fair hero is given to me!"
   Now hear what the clever fellow said
As soon as he heard whom she would wed.
2235 "If Rother is the lucky man,
I'll bring him here as fast as I can.
There doesn't live a man today
Who treated me in a better way —
For which he will always have my thanks —
2240 Until he was ridden by arrogance.
He helped me often in time of need —
For which may God give him his meed!
We dwelled together in the land
And happily lived as lord and man.
2245 He always was gracious and good to me,
Though now in exile I must be."
The princess said: "From what I hear,
It wasn't Rother (that is clear!)
Who drove you hither, hero true,
2250 Seeing he's so revered by you.
From whencesoever you do fare,
You've come as an envoy to us, I swear!
The king's good will you cherish so!
Now tell me all I want to know.
2255 Whatever today is said to me
I shall keep secret faithfully
Even to the Judgment Day."
Thereupon the lord did say:
"To God I now commend my life
2260 And to you also, gentle wife.
Your feet are lying, I avow,
In the lap of Rother now!"
   How very great was her dismay!
At once she pulled her feet away
2265 And said to him with eyes downcast
(Truly, she was much abashed!):
"By my pride I've been misled.
Never was I so ill-bred.
It was of me most indiscreet
2270 To put upon your lap my feet.
But if Rother really is your name,

    Then you can never, O King, attain
To greater merit than you have now.
Of many wonderful things, I vow,
2275 You have achieved the mastery,
Whatever may be your pedigree.
My heart had a presentiment!
And if by God you have been sent,
Then that will give me much delight.
2280 But I cannot believe it quite
Until you prove that it is so.
Then though it cause the whole world woe,
I certainly shall have no fear
In running off with you from here.
2285 But without the proof that may not be.
Yet no man lives so splendidly
That I would take him ahead of you
If what you've said is really true."
    Thus did Dieterich reply
2290 (Truly, he was very sly):
"I am bereft of every friend
Excepting for those wretched men
Who are lying here in captivity.
If they were to get a glimpse of me,
2295 From their behavior you would know
That what I've said is really so."
Then said the princess: "Verily,
I'll get my father to agree
To let those men go free a while:
2300 I'll manage that with a little guile.
But he won't surrender their custody
Except to the man who can guarantee
That missing will be none of them
When it shall be time once again
2305 To bring them into that dungeon bare
Where they so wretchedly do fare."
    Said Dieterich: "If it must be,
I'm ready to stand surety.
Tomorrow I intend to dine
2310 Here at the court of Constantine.
You can believe that I speak the truth!"
Thereupon the handsome youth
Got from the lovely maid a kiss.
And so with honor he was dismissed.
2315 Then over the yard he went apace
To where he had his lodging-place.

As soon as Berchter noticed that,
He quickly called the giants back.
From Rother then the good duke heard
2320 Everything that had occurred.
His heart was filled with great delight.
They both began to praise God's might.
    All night the damsel lay awake.
What a heavy turn her thoughts did take!
2325 As soon as dawn came to the land,
She took a staff into her hand
And dressed herself in garments dun
Like one who has become a nun.
Then over her shoulder a palm-leaf she put
2330 As if she would go from the land on foot.
Quickly then the maiden went
To Constantine's apartment.
Upon the little door she knocked.
By her father then it was unlocked.
2335 As soon as she had been let in,
How cleverly she said to him:
"I'm at your service, father dear!
Mother mine, be of good cheer!
Now listen to what this night I dreamt!
2340 Unless Almighty God consent
To send his angel down to me,
In the abyss I needs must be
Even before my life runs out —
Of that there can't be any doubt!
2345 Now no one can make me change my plan
Of dwelling in a foreign land
So that for my sins I may atone
As long as this world is still my home!"
    Sadly then said Constantine:
2350 "Do not speak so, daughter mine!
Let me know what you desire.
I'll save you from eternal fire."
"Father, that can never be
Unless the envoys are given to me.
2355 I wish to have them bathed and clad,
So that once more each wretched lad
May feel contented enough to smile —
If only for a little while.
For three days I would care for them.
2360 Then they'll be given back again
To be imprisoned once more by you."

The mighty Emperor said thereto
That he would do that willingly
If she found someone to agree
2365 To pledge his life that the wretched men
Would be returned to him again
Without a single one having fled.
To this the lovely maiden said:
"So many men today I'll ask
2370 That someone will accept the task
Who lives so honestly that you may
Give them to him without dismay."
Then Constantine replied thereto:
"Daughter, that I'll gladly do."
2375   As soon as it was time to dine,
One saw the Emperor Constantine
Make his way into the hall.
Then Dieterich did not wait at all:
Together with his following
2380 He hurried there before the king.
As soon as they had begun to dine,
The lovely maiden came betime
And started to walk around the table,
Weeping as sorely as she was able
2385 And asking who of them would agree
To offer himself as surety
Against the return of the envoys fair.
Not one of them dared to grant her prayer.
Even the great dukes were afraid
2390 To offer the maiden any aid.
At last she drew near to the man
With whom she had worked out her plan.
To him the damsel said anon:
"Sir Dieterich, now think upon
2395 The excellent qualities you possess
And rescue me from my distress!
Go surety for the envoys fair:
The king will give them into your care.
Faint-hearted are my father's men:
2400 Not one will risk his life for them.
But you, dear sir, will honor me
By letting me share your nobility
So that I may have the benefit.
Even though you would refrain from it,
2405 Your excellence wouldn't allow you to.
You shall vouchsafe it, hero true!"

    Dieterich answered: "Willingly,
Since it is you who ask it of me.
It's only my life that will be at stake.
2410 I'll do it, fair damsel, for your sake."
    Constantine set the envoys free
Against Sir Dieterich's guarantee:
Into his charge he delivered them.
Together with the Emperor's men
2415 He hastened thither to the cell
Where they were lying, so we hear tell.
The wretched men lay on the ground:
They were too weak to move around.
It was a sight to make one weep!
2420 The mighty Berchter could not keep
From shedding many a bitter tear
When their lamenting reached his ear.
The dungeon-door was opened wide.
Swiftly the daylight fell inside.
2425 It struck upon the prisoners' eyes.
They started blinking in surprise.
    Erwin was the first of the men
To step forth from the dungeon then.
When Berchter caught sight of his son,
2430 With anguish he was overcome.
He quickly turned his face away
And wrung his hands in his dismay.
He did not dare to express his woe.
And yet he may never have suffered so
2435 Since he first saw the light of day.
Erwin was in a pitiful way!
He hardly had the strength to stand.
Truly, he was a wretched man!
    The twelve counts soon came into view,
2440 Followed by their vassals true.
Now our story will let you hear
Just how the good lads did appear.
Black and dirty was every knight,
All discolored by their plight.
2445 On Master Lupold, so we're told,
Nothing else could one behold
Except a wretched little breech
Which round his waist could hardly reach.
The unhappy fellow was indeed
2450 A picture of the direst need—
Bruised and swollen everywhere!

Dieterich, the hero fair,
Stood there overcome with grief;
Yet tears might bring him no relief:
2455 He dared not betray the valiant band.
The ancient Berchter then began
To walk around the captive men,
Carefully observing them.
Nothing had ever grieved him so
2460 As the plight of his handsome sons, I trow!
   Sir Dieterich commanded then
That one should lead the noblemen
To his abode without delay;
Lupold and Erwin alone might stay.
2465 One let them walk about in the air
Without anyone to guard the pair.
The noble Erwin then did say:
"Master Lupold, tell me, pray,
If you can make out over there
2470 An ancient man with a beard so fair
Who all the time kept watching me
As if he were troubled wondrously.
From me he turned his face away
And wrung his hands in great dismay.
2475 He didn't dare to express his woe,
And yet he may never have suffered so.
What if Almighty God above,
In token of His lasting love,
Intends to give us now a sign
2480 That we shall come from here in time?
Brother dear, it seems to me
That our good father he well may be."
Then both began to laugh aloud.
Happy and sad were the heroes proud.
2485   The wretched men were set at large,
Given into Dieterich's charge.
On the morning of the second day
The damsel asked her sire to say
That she might go and see the men:
2490 She wished herself to care for them.
When he had given his consent,
How quickly over the yard she went
To the noble Dieterich's dwelling-place.
Then all the knights of a foreign race
2495 Were asked by him to go outside.
None of the gentlemen might abide

     Who wasn't of the closest kin
     And had sailed across the sea for him.
     The handsome envoys then were clad
2500 In the finest raiment to be had
     And given armor of the best:
     This was at Dieterich's behest.
     The tables were covered with food anon.
     One put Sir Berchter thereupon
2505 In charge of both the food and wine
     As long as his sons were pleased to dine.
        When all the knights had been seated there
     And had forgotten some of their care,
     The noble Dieterich stepped apart
2510 And came back with an excellent harp.
     Then he sneaked behind the tapestry.
     How quickly rang out a melody!
     Those who had begun to drink
     Had to let their beakers sink,
2515 So that on the table the wine was shed.
     Those who were busy cutting the bread
     Had no choice but to drop their knives:
     They lost their wits from glad surmise.
     ... ...
     How many put on a cheerful guise!
2520 Everyone could hardly wait
     To hear what turn the music would take.
     Loudly then a melody sounded.
     Over the table Lupold bounded,
     Followed by Count Erwin then.
2525 How warmly did the noblemen
     Salute the harpist of high degree
     And kiss him most decorously!
     The damsel then could clearly see
     That the noble Rother he must be.
2530   As soon as the damsel had turned from there,
     The envoys were allowed to fare
     Everywhere in the famous town
     Without anyone to follow them round.
     When Constantine's men got wind of this,
2535 They told him that something was amiss.
     He answered: "Do not be concerned!
     Dieterich pledged that they'd be returned.

   L. 2518 Here a line is probably missing in which mention was made of the playing of the second melody.

His intellect is so very keen
That none will get away, I ween!"
2540   Upon the bidding of the queen
One began to sweep the dungeon clean.
When three full days had come and gone,
The messengers were seized anon
And brought into the dungeon-cell,
2545 Where they once more were forced to dwell.
Of bedding then a goodly store
And other nice things by the score
Were smuggled in to them secretly;
And so most comfortable they might be.
2550 Wheaten rolls and white bread, too,
Tasted good to the heroes true.
The damsel then dispatched a man
To Dieterich with a clever plan.
He bade his followers then prepare
2555 A tunnel leading to the air
… … … … … … … … … … … … …
Whenever they wished to go from there.
And so the prisoners reclined
In a contented frame of mind.
They lay at ease there in the hold
2560 For twenty days, so we are told,
And wanted nothing for their board.
To vigor then they were restored.
   Beneath the heavens arose meantime
Against the Emperor Constantine
2565 Princes two-and-seventy strong
From the land of Egyptian Babylon.
They rode at the head of the mightiest band
That had ventured forth from any land.
Ymelot, a paynim king,
2570 Was determined to capture him.
Nothing could stand in his way.
He wanted to extend his sway
Over the kingdoms one by one.
Throughout the whole of heathendom
2575 His commands were greatly feared.
Like God he wanted to be revered.
(Similin was the name of his wife.
At Jerusalem later he lost his life.)

L. 2555 A line is probably missing here.
L. 2566 *Egyptian Babylon* — Cairo.

      In haste a man came riding then
2580 Ahead of the terrible Ymelot's men
To Constantinople Town,
The citadel of great renown,
And let it be known to Constantine
That there was very little time
2585 If the didn't want to be overrun—
To his realm a mighty host had come!
Constantine said thereupon:
"What man ever was so strong
That he would dare invade my land?"
2590 Now hear the reply of the hurrying man:
"Your overweening pride, my lord,
Is something you cannot afford.
That's just what they are doing now!
It is King Ymelot, I vow,
2595 From the land of Egyptian Babylon.
Princes two-and-seventy strong
Are riding here in hostile wise.
I saw the van with my own eyes.
So many tents have they pitched, I swear,
2600 That a hundred thousand may well be there!"
      As soon as Constantine heard this news,
His spirits he began to lose.
Then Dieterich, the hero good,
Cheered him up as best he could.
2605 He said: "Despair not, Constantine!
I'll pledge to you this life of mine
If you will give those men to me
Who are lying here in captivity.
If horses and armor they only had,
2610 They'd furnish many a valiant lad.
Now gather your followers straight away:
We must ride forth without delay."
"May God reward you," the king replied.
"My chamberlains have set aside
2615 Both the horses and the gear
With which the envoys traveled here.
They'll get it back again all right,
Seeing that you, most worthy knight,
Have pledged your word to stand by me
2620 Now that I need help so desperately."
      Constantine agreed to do
As Dieterich had advised him to.
He sent his messengers far and wide.

Then many brave men began to ride
2625 To Constantinople Town,
The citadel of great renown,
So that before three days had passed
Fifty thousand he had amassed.
Thereupon the heroes bold
2630 Hurried thither to the hold
And let the door be opened wide
And had the twelve counts brought outside
Together with their trusty men.
Quickly one gave back to them
2635 What they had brought across the sea.
The valiant Dieterich speedily
Received them all into his troop
And fitted them out from head to foot.
They mounted steeds that were snowy white.
2640 Then filled with hope was the worthy knight.
    The youthful men set out apace.
Upon their steeds they began to race.
Twenty thousand warriors bold
Behind Sir Dieterich's banner rode
2645 In armor shining through the land.
Under Constantine's command
Many a brave lad rode along
To defend the realm from the paynim throng.
For seven nights, our story tells,
2650 They rode to meet the infidels.
    The princes two-and-seventy strong
From the land of Egyptian Babylon
Pitched their tents so near to them
That they were able to make out then
2655 The smoke from the camp-fires rising clear.
Then many a man was seized by fear.
Then Dieterich cheered up the lot:
He pitched his tent in the foremost spot,
Right between the armies twain.
2660 His valiant followers did the same.
    The day drew swiftly to an end.
Constantine's troops began to commend
To one another their children and wives:
They feared lest they might lose their lives.
2665 Dieterich and his trusty men
Stealthily went walking then
And plotted against the paynim throng
Who were lying there with an army strong.

       They pictured how great would be their fame
2670   If the famous Ymelot should be slain
       Or taken prisoner by them
       Without losing any of Constantine's men.
       Then Widolt said: "I'm willing to swear
       That when we come among them there
2675   I shan't be overly circumspect,
       Seeing that Christ they do reject.
       But this much I can guarantee,
       That if my hands shall be set free
       Some of them will dearly pay!"
2680   Then Asprian armed himself straightway,
       And twelve good knights who knew no fear
       Slipped into their battle-gear.
       Eager were they for the fray!
       Then a corselet shone as bright as day;
2685   It was worn by the hero Asprian.
       There never lived so bold a man
       But with his life would have to pay
       If he were ever to cross his way
       Among the paynim host, I swear.
2690   Mightily they rose up there.
           Then Berchter issued a command
       To all the men in Dieterich's band
       To keep a careful lookout
       And raise their voices in a shout.
2695   Said he: "My lord and his trusty crew
       Have with the king a rendezvous:
       Constantine has sent for them."
       Many a doughty hero then
       In goodly armor could be seen.
2700   No one knew about the scheme
       Excepting those of the nearest kin
       Who had sailed across the sea for him.
           To the horses Dieterich went anon.
       Then above a handsome steed there shone
2705   A golden hauberk through the land.
       It was worn by the most ferocious man
       Who ever drew a breath of air
       Since God made Adam, I declare!
       A terrible club was in his hand
2710   Before which not a thing could stand.
       Then heartened by him was Dieterich's crew.
       Widolt it was, a hero true.
           The faithful Lupold then began

To warn the giants to a man:
2715 "Clad in your corselets shining so,
From our midst beware to go
Lest you should throw too great a glare."
Then Dieterich rode with his men from there
And circled around the paynim throng
2720 Who were lying there with an army strong.
He asked whomever he did see
Where the Emperor Ymelot might be:
He had been detained in getting there
And was bringing many a hero fair.
2725 From one to another he was sent
Until he came to a splendid tent
In which was lying the paynim lord.
Asprian then unsheathed his sword
And bade him not to blink an eye
2730 Unless it was his wish to die.
Ymelot didn't make a sound
When he saw the club being swung around.
It seemed to him a terrible thing!
Captured then was the mighty king.
2735   Dieterich and his trusty men
Proceeded with great valor then.
They fell upon a compact group
And laid low the entire troop.
Widolt refused to give away
2740 His club to anyone that day.
Whatever paynims crossed his path
He struck like thunder in his wrath.
Whenever he came into the press
He hit them with such ruthlessness
2745 That their defence was shattered
Like dust that the wind has scattered.
   The twelve fierce giants then began
To take the life of many a man.
The paynim troops were forced to flee
2750 With Death pursuing them pitilessly.
Widolt was restrained once more,
Fettered as he had been before.
Thereupon Sir Dieterich went
Back to the encampment
2755 And showed to everyone a face
As though nothing at all had taken place.
   Dieterich bade his noble crew
Return to camp without ado

   And leave their horses undisturbed,
2760 No matter what clamor might be heard.
   Then from the sentry at his post
   A cry went over all the host:
   "Rise up now, Lord Constantine!
   There is coming to these ears of mine
2765 A mighty clamor from the foe.
   They're starting to attack, I trow!"
   Ah! how terrible was their fright
   As soon as they heard the sound of flight
   Coming from the paynim throng,
2770 Who were lying there with an army strong.
   To don his armor Constantine ran,
   And with him many a valiant man.
   Then some of his followers said to him:
   "Now look at Dieterich, O King!
2775 He doesn't stir out of craven fear,
   Although it was he who led us here.
   O Constantine, it's plain to see
   That you've been undone by his treachery."
    Constantine jumped on his steed
2780 And rode off with the greatest speed
   To where a splendid tent was pitched.
   "Rise up now, Sir Dieterich!
   We're being attacked by the paynim band.
   Death draws near for many a man!"
2785 Then in a loud voice Ymelot spoke:
   "Sir, there is no need to joke.
   Last night, ere the break of day,
   As sleeping on my couch I lay,
   A terrible man came in to me
2790 And carried me off bodily.
   My retinue have all been slain.
   They cannot harm you ever again."
    As soon as Constantine heard of this,
   He turned away from there full of bliss
2795 And told the news to his following.
   "Captured is the paynim king!
   For this must Dieterich be acclaimed.
   Now everyone must be ashamed
   Who ever talked to the despite
2800 Of such a very worthy knight
   Wrongfully and without cause."
   Then many a good lad did not pause
   But hastened to where Dieterich stood

And expressed his thanks as best he could.
2805 Constantine jumped from his horse and went
Ahead of his men into the tent.
He stretched his hands out to the knight.
"May God Almighty now requite
Both you and your following
2810 For having captured the paynim king.
Upon my honor, worthy lord,
How glorious will be your reward!
If there is anything of mine
Which you may wish to have some time,
2815 You only have to ask for it."
Of all their worries they were quit.
   As soon as day came to the land,
One handed over many a man.
Dieterich did not delay:
2820 He led King Ymelot straight away
Into the presence of Constantine
And handed him over to him betime.
The clever man said thereupon:
"An envoy we must have anon
2825 To ride and let the ladies hear
All that we have accomplished here."
Then Constantine replied thereto:
"In truth, that envoy shall be you!
'Twill please my daughter well, I ween.
2830 And make it known to my wife the queen
And to all the other ladies, too,
How joyfully we follow you
Back to our native land again.
Now give instructions to some of your men
2835 That here with me they must abide."
The clever fellow then replied
That he would very gladly do
Whatever the king desired him to.
Dieterich departed then
2840 Together with his trusty men.
He sent his army to Constantine
And thanked them all full many a time.
No other men did he retain
Save those who had sailed across the main.
2845 Then he revealed to his valiant crew
Just what it was he planned to do.
Then hope arose in the doughty band
Of seeing once more their native land.

No time at all did Dieterich waste:
2850 With a splendid banner he rode in haste
Back to Constantinople Town,
The citadel of great renown.
The clever fellow then did say
That with his men he had run away.
2855 At this the queen wept bitterly.
"Alas, where now may Constantine be,
And where may be that valiant band
Which gathered here from many a land?
Tell me, Dieterich, I implore!
2860 Shall we ever see them more?"
"Upon my word, to hope were vain.
By Ymelot they've all been slain.
With an army he is riding here
And means to destroy the town, I fear.
2865 I think he is too strong for me!
Now I shall sail across the sea.
Both the children and the wives
Must prepare to lose their lives
If in the town they do remain —
2870 By Ymelot they will be slain!"
   Constantine's wife led with her there
Her daughter (she was a maiden fair),
And both implored the worthy knight
Just as urgently as they might
2875 To save them from the heathen throng
Who were riding there with an army strong.
The crafty fellow ordered then
The palfreys brought at once to them,
And he led the queen and her daughter, too,
2880 Down to the ships without more ado.
Truly, there could then be seen
Ladies of most lovely mien
Weeping aloud and tearing their hair:
They had to give vent to their despair.
2885 Behind Sir Dieterich went along
From out the town a migthy throng.
It was the hope of all those wives
That on the sea they might save their lives.
The clever man did not dissent.
2890 It all was done with sly intent.
   The noble Dieterich bade his men
Swiftly board the vessels then.
Asprian, the hero bold,

Brought the treasure into the hold.
2895 They wished to reach the open sea.
Then King Rother did decree
That the mother be left upon the shore
And the daughter be taken and no one more.
Then many a tear the old queen shed.
2900 "Alas, Sir Dieterich," she pled,
"To whom would you, most worthy knight,
Abandon us women in our plight?"
Further did the good queen say:
"Take me into your ship, I pray,
2905 That I may be at my daughter's side."
The clever fellow then replied:
"Madam, you need not complain!
Constantine has not been slain.
We've captured the mighty infidel.
2910 For Constantine it's turned out well.
He is riding back to his kingdom now,
Bringing pleasant news, I vow.
In three days' time he will be here.
Now you can tell him without fear
2915 That westward does King Rother ride
With his fair daughter by his side.
Now God preserve you, gentle dame!
Dieterich is not my name."
"O happy me," the queen did say,
2920 "That ever I saw the light of day!
Now may Almighty God above,
In token of His lasting love,
Let you keep my daughter dear
Free from sorrow many a year.
2925 Worthy man, I tell you true:
It wouldn't have been so hard for you
To win the maiden for your own
If the choice were up to me alone.
Now though the king will tear his hair
2930 When he hears about his daughter fair,
That isn't going to bother me,
Now that Rother you've proved to be.
Be on your way now, hero true,
And may Saint Aegidius watch over you!"
2935 Then said the lovely demoiselle:
"Mother mine, God keep you well!"
Thereupon the ladies fair
Laughing merrily went from there

            Back to the palace of Constantine
2940   And wished for Rother many a time
            That God might bring him over the main
            With honor to his own domain.
               As soon as Rother came back home
            Sailing west across the foam,
2945   His lovely wife did then become
            Pregnant with a blessed son.
            By that time Amalger was dead,
            From all the realm had order fled.
            For that six margraves were to blame
2950   Because they wanted to proclaim
            Hadamar as King of Rome.
            (In Diessen was the lord at home,
            And he was a great duke, verily.)
            Those who had pledged their loyalty
2955   To Rother while he was away
            Defended the crown for many a day
            On behalf of their mighty errant lord
            Till Wolfrat was knighted with the sword,
            Standing in a splendid ring.
2960   (He was the lord of Tengeling
            And was, in truth, King Amalger's son.
            Never from one line has come
            Such a host of heroes fair.)
            The worthy man defended there
2965   Both the people and the throne
            Until King Rother came back home.
               In strife lay all the countryside.
            The valiant Rother might not bide.
            He gave his travel-weary men
2970   No chance to rest their bodies then:
            He had to bring order to his land.
            The faithful Lupold he did command
            To guard the ladies while he was gone.
            The other good knights thereupon
2975   Mounted their steeds in full array.
            Many an honest lad that day
            Galloped over the mountainside.
            To Verona with their king they hied.
            The giants in their battle-gear
2980   Ran beside them, so we hear.
            Wolfrat shared in the enterprise:

   L. 2952 *Diessen* — a market-town in Upper Bavaria.

                An army of tremendous size
                He led with him across the land
                To join up with King Rother's band.
2985   He greeted with respect his lord,
                As with his honor it did accord.
                   Because the clamor was so great,
                A crowd began to congregate
                When Constantine with his followers came
2990   Riding back to the court amain
                At Constantinople in the town.
                Hastily he asked around
                Where might be his daughter fair,
                Since he didn't see her anywhere.
2995   To this the queen his wife replied:
                "O Constantine, be satisfied!
                That nobleman so excellent
                Who by the name of Dieterich went —
                King Rother is his name, I swear!
3000   Now he has led our daughter fair
                Westward over the sea with him.
                How better wedded could she have been?
                The clever fellow said to me
                That he'll keep her for surety
3005   Until such time as he is paid
                For having rendered you his aid.
                Properly has he treated us.
                It all was too ridiculous!
                What exile ever had such might?
3010   Constantine, take this aright!
                If an exile should come to your shore,
                Take better heed than heretofore!"
                   When Constantine learned what had passed,
                His pleasant humor did not last.
3015   He started to weep and carry on so;
                He beat his breast from heartfelt woe.
                Said he: "Ah, madam, what grief is mine!
                For my daughter I shall always pine
                Whom Rother snatched away from me
3020   And led with him across the sea.
                How dearly have I had to pay
                For all that he did give away!"
                From grief he fell into a swound.
                Then in great numbers from the town

3025 The citizens came hurrying nigh.
      ... ...
      They raised aloft a mighty cry.
      How Ymelot was helped thereby!
      The man who had to look after him
      Ran off to inquire about the din;
3030 Truly, he could not forgo
      Learning why they were shouting so.
      Then Ymelot did not delay:
      He saved himself in a clever way.
      While Constantine lay in a swound,
3035 Ymelot ran out of town.
      In a vessel then he managed to flee
      With a band of merchants over the sea
      To the land of Egyptian Babylon.
      Many a prince had later on
3040 To suffer for his sake grievous pain.
      To the heroes too much trouble came.
         When Constantine regained his wits,
      Then all the folk, both poor and rich,
      Started to shout in their dismay:
3045 "Ymelot has run away!"
      "Woe is me!" said Constantine.
      "Now take the treasure, mistress mine,
      And share it with the valiant men
      And help them to their homes again,
3050 So that retainers I shan't lack
      In case King Ymelot does attack."
      She didn't stint with the gold a bit:
      She covered all their shields with it.
      To every prince of high degree
3055 She gave of it right liberally,
      And rewarded every honest knight.
      (Just so today one strives aright
      To earn for himself a glorious name.)
      Homeward then they fared amain.
3060   When all that mighty gathering
      Had left the presence of the king,
      To him a minstrel then did say:
      "Sire, I wish you health alway!
      If you will reward me, Constantine,
3065 I'll bring your daughter back betime.
      But for that we need to have a ship

L. 3025 A line is missing here.

With all sorts of wondrous things in it:
Gold and jewels to please the eyes,
Genuine pearls of dainty size,
3070 Satins and silks for the ladies fair,
So that whoever would purchase there
Will find that we are well supplied.
And with us sixty knights must ride
Who shall keep hidden all the time.
3075 The precious stuffs, O Constantine,
Will captivate the damsel so
That into the ship she'll quickly go
To take a look at my display.
Then with her we shall sail away!
3080 Now tell me what my reward shall be;
And if your offer pleases me,
Then I will gladly lose my life
If I don't bring you Rother's wife."
   Said Constantine: "I thank you, sir!
3085 Now to my treasure I refer.
Help yourself, good friend, to it
Just as freely as you think fit.
I'm eager to see this journey made.
Be sure that you'll be well repaid!"
3090 At once the rigging on the ship
Was got in readiness for the trip.
The ruddy gold was brought aboard
At the behest of the mighty lord.
Rings and pins and bows for the hair,
3095 Stuffs for clothes exceeding rare
Constantine provided then
To get his daughter back again.
One began to bring the wares on board.
Everything was quickly stored.
3100 The clever minstrel and his crew
Sailed away without more ado
To the town of Bari by the sea.
At that time Rother had to be
In the Rhineland, so we're told,
3105 Together with his heroes bold.
There he saw that justice was done
To the widows and orphans every one.
   As soon as the accursed Greeks
Had moored their vessel on the beach,
3110 The minstrel straightway went ashore
And brought back with him pebbles four

>
> Which he had found upon the strand.
> How clever was the devilish man!
> Now hear just what he wanted to do
> 3115 Or whom he wanted to sell them to!
>   Next morning at the break of day
> The minstrel put upon display
> A quantity of fabrics rare
> In a stall that he had erected there.
> 3120 The burghers then came out on foot:
> They were very eager to have a look.
> They bargained there for silks and gold.
> "For how much, friend, might that be sold?"
> Nothing was so richly wrought
> 3125 But for a penny it could be bought.
> The burghers then were ready to swear
> That they had a fool to deal with there.
> Whatever goods were on display
> They bought from him without delay.
> 3130 One of them saw the pebbles then.
> "How much for one of those, good friend?"
> Then he said that it might not be sold
> For less than a thousand pounds of gold
> Of such an excellent quality
> 3135 As might suit a lady of high degree.
> In reply to this the burgher said:
> "You're only trying to pull my leg.
> You must be one of the Devil's own.
> It looks to me like a common stone!"
> 3140   The minstrel answered: "Now I swear
> That to this stone you are not fair!
> You ought not to abuse it so.
> For many things it's good, I trow.
> If a queen should take it in her hand
> 3145 It would shine out over all the land.
> Supposing that someone had died
> And had not yet been laid aside:
> If he were stroked with this stone here
> He'd rise up quickly, never fear!
> 3150 There is no one so crippled or lame
> But he would quickly walk again
> If the queen were to touch him a single time
> With this most excellent stone of mine.
> But she has to do it in the ship,
> 3155 Else he will have no good of it.
> If we had a cripple now, my lord,

And the queen were willing to go on board,
Then if what I have been telling you
Should turn out to have been untrue,
3160 You may bid your men take hold of me
And hang me from the nearest tree."
    Then to the minstrel said a knight
(Great in Bari was his might):
"I am the father of children twain
3165 Who for a year now have been lame,
So that we must carry them everywhere.
Now to the queen I will repair.
Perhaps of her goodness she'll agree
To cure them of their infirmity.
3170 If they are aided by your stone
So that they're able to walk back home,
With so much wealth I'll gladly pay
As you may be able to carry away."
"If I am lying," the minstrel said,
3175 "Let your men cut off my head!
But I don't fear such a penalty:
My life is much too dear to me."
Then he gathered all his kinsmen round —
Sixteen merchants of the town —
3180 And to the queen he did repair.
He was welcomed by the lady fair
In a manner very debonair —
Just as if he were someone
Who from a princely line did come.
3185   Then he hastened to entreat her
In the name of good Saint Peter
To do whatever she could to save
Two victims of an ailment grave.
"They are my children, gracious dame,
3190 Who for a long time have been lame.
A ship is lying in the bay
To which I'll bring them straight away.
Excellent stones are there on board
By which the sick can be restored.
3195 If you were to take one in your hand,
It would shine forth over all the land.
Supposing that someone had died
And had not yet been laid aside:
If you should stroke him then with it,
3200 At once he'd rise up perfectly fit.
There is no one so crippled or lame

      But would be quickly sound again,
      As that lad gave us to understand
      Who brought these pebbles to our land.
3205 He says, if what I'm telling you
      Should turn out to have been untrue,
      Then it will be all right for me
      To hang him from the nearest tree.
      For God's sake try it, gracious dame!
3210 A rich reward you well may claim
      If you can heal those sons of mine
      Who have been lame so long a time.
      What pain it brings to wretched me
      When I behold their misery!"
3215   Now hear the answer the queen did make!
      "Since you entreat me for Jesus' sake,
      I find I must agree to it.
      Let them be carried to the ship!"
      At that time Lupold was away.
3220 Then twenty good knights did not delay:
      They went to the ship with the lady fair.
      Quickly one brought the sick lads there,
      Whose health was going to be restored.
      As soon as the lady stepped on board,
3225 "Let us be off!" the minstrel cried.
      "To the land of Greece it's time to ride!
      That woman for whom we made this trip —
      Behold her standing in the ship!"
      Then all the Greeks with one accord
3230 Swiftly made their way on board.
      They threw the sick lads back on land.
      No one got stroked by the good queen's hand.
      Those who were waiting on the dame
      Were led by the Greeks across the main.
3235 Now take a look at that devilish man —
      How he had succeeded with his plan!
        The Greeks sailed quickly on their way.
      The lady bade the minstrel say
      At whose behest he and his band
3240 Had journeyed thither to that land.
      "In truth, it was Lord Constantine,
      Your dear father, mistress mine,
      Who ordered us to cross the sea."
      "Alas, King Rother, woe is me!"
3245 The wretched woman cried aloud.
      "Henceforth upon your body proud

You will inflict the direst pain.
For your sake I shall do the same."
　　The lady was in a pitiful state.
3250 The minstrel had her carried straight
To Constantinople Town.
How quickly then the news spread round
That success had crowned their prince's plan!
Then all the burghers to a man
3255 Welcomed the queen with one accord.
Quickly Constantine went on board..
He took his daughter by the hand
And escorted her onto the land.
He hugged her and he kissed her.
3260 How sorely he had missed her!
Her mother drew nigh weeping:
She did not like this meeting.
No matter what the old queen said,
Her daughter only bowed her head.
3265 Constantine was full of cheer.
To all her words he lent no ear.
He let his daughter hold her peace
Until she had enough of grief.
　　The news began to spread around
3270 Everywhere in Bari Town
That the lady had been snatched away.
Then they feared lest Rother would make them pay.
Then all the townsfolk, men and wives,
Hoped by fleeing to save their lives.
3275 Then Lupold hurried to them anon
And cheered up the downhearted throng.
He pleaded with them not to flee
And said that he could guarantee
That Rother's anger would abate,
3280 So that he would not seek to take
Revenge on anyone for the blame,
Nor say anything to cause them shame.
The wealthy burghers all alike
Fell at the feet of the worthy knight.
3285 They promised him that they would do
Whatsoever he asked them to —
They depended fully on his aid.
Truly, they were much afraid!
Then said the very worthy knight:
3290 "God will rescue us from our plight.
So great is my master's loyalty,

     We may yet be saved if God so decree."
       Seven nights from that same day
     Rother came with great array
3295 Riding back to Bari Town
     And heard some news that cast him down.
     The faithful Lupold went apace
     And took his stand in the foremost place.
     Then said the hero unafraid:
3300 "Noble lord, I have betrayed
     The confidence you showed in me.
     Your wife is back beyond the sea!
     The Emperor Constantine has, alas,
     Brought that cleverly to pass.
3305 Your anger, sire, must be so great
     That now my life you'll want to take.
     My brother Erwin is here with me.
     He lay in Greek captivity
     On your account a weary time
3310 And forgot how it was for the sun to shine.
     Now give us for this our just reward
     By sparing these people, worthy lord.
     They have been blameless all along;
     They have not done you any wrong.
3315 'Twas I who encouraged them to stay
     When they were bent on running away.
     I urged them all to tarry
     Here with me in Bari.
     The blame is mine alone to bear.
3320 Sentence me now, hero fair,
     As is only proper and right.
     Tell me why an honest knight
     Should have any further need of wealth
     If he has not kept faith with himself.
3325 Now since I haven't done so,
     Out of this world I'm ready to go."
       Now hear how the mighty Rother spoke,
     Who had been dealt this grievous stroke!
     There before that noble band
3330 He took Sir Lupold by the hand
     And paid him honor with a kiss.
     "Cousin, think no more of this!
     You have no reason to be dismayed.
     There still lives many a lovely maid.
3335 But if the lady was meant to be
     A source of happiness to me,

Then it may finally come out right.
No more of this, most worthy knight!
If you were now to feel my rage,
3340 That would be indeed a sorry wage
For the service you often rendered me.
You lay in Greek captivity
Eighteen months, O hero fair,
And of your life you did despair,
3345 And with you many a hero true.
If I were ever wroth with you,
Like Judas I should be to blame,
Who condemned himself to eternal shame.
Now tell these burghers standing here
3350 That they have nothing at all to fear."
    Many an honest fellow saw
How the king conceived the law
And how his anger had been meant.
Thereupon Sir Berchter went
3355 Just as politely as he could
To where the noble Rother stood,
And burst out laughing from delight.
"May God allow me to requite
The mercy you have shown my son.
3360 For my poor sake 'twas surely done.
You have today, O hero bold,
Renewed the excellent way of old
Which by your father were highly prized
As long as he was still alive.
3365 If now my body were only so
As it was fifty years ago,
I'd repay this honor you have done
As well as many another one.
But now, alas, that may not be!
3370 Constantine has recently
Been most unkind to some of you.
Never forget that, heroes true —
You who here before us stand.
He is, in truth, a devilish man!
3375 Rother, my advice would be
To fare in force across the sea.
This beard of mine is not so grey
That here at home I'd consent so stay!"
    "Where are now," said Asprian then,
3380 "My master Rother's loyal men,
With whom it was his pleasure

          To share his wealth and treasure —
          Now that he needs them in his plight?"
          One saw then many a worthy knight
3385 Push his way into the ring.
          … … … … … … … … … … … …
          And the right to many a great estate.
          And so they did not hesitate
          To swear unto their mighty lord,
          As with their honor it did accord,
3390 That if he ever were bestead
          They'd fight for him till they were dead.
          In a loud voice Widolt shouted then:
          "Here is a splendid band of men!
          They're not afraid, it's plain to see,
3395 Of losing kin and property,
          Rother, to preserve your fame.
          We'll help you come across the main!
          Whoever renders service true
          Will be rewarded well by you.
3400 Constantine's followers were not slow
          To deal us a most grievous blow.
          If we don't repay it 'twould be a shame.
          My trouble would have been all in vain."
             Then up spoke Wolfrat, a hero proud:
3405 "Seeing that Widolt now has vowed
          That we shall help His Majesty
          To make a trip across the sea,
          I shall lead forth from my own land
          To join the rest a mighty band
3410 Of heroes dauntless in the fray —
          Twelve thousand knights in fine array.
          I swear that I shall help maintain
          The name of Lupold free from shame.
          The gentleman and I are kin.
3415 It is indeed a Christian thing
          When brothers and cousins all agree
          To live together honorably.
          Whoever abandons one of his kin
          When things aren't going well for him —
3420 Had he left a countryman in the lurch,
          His honor would be less besmirched.
          The noble Rother did behave
          As well becomes a hero brave:

L. 3385 One or more lines are missing here.

After my father had been banned,
3425 He helped win back for him his land.
By him Duke Elbewin was slain
(From the region of the Rhine he came
And he was, in truth, a terrible foe
Who often caused us grievous woe).
3430 Because of the love we bear him now,
Cousin Lupold, I do vow
That you can count upon my aid
As long as I can swing a blade!"
Thus spoke proudly in the ring
3435 The worthy lord of Tengeling.
    The valiant Lupold then did say:
"Vassals and kinsmen, where are they?
Verily, we must cross the main
To the Emperor Constantine's domain.
3440 Cousin Wolfrat, set out now
In accordance with your vow.
Ride home now to your domain
And call up many a doughty thane.
And I shall likewise lead apace
3445 Young lads to the gathering-place
From the city of Milan,
Which I have as King Rother's man —
Twenty thousand keen to fight,
Clad in hauberks shining bright.
3450 Let us set a time, I pray:
Twelve weeks from this very day,
Here at Bari by the sea."
Then many a lad swore willingly
An oath unto their mighty lord,
3455 As with their honor it did accord.
    The Duke of Meran then did swear:
"Twenty thousand heroes fair,
Rother, you shall have from me
To help you come across the sea.
3460 And this I furthermore do say:
If Constantine should cross my way,
My sword will deal him such a blow
That he will never recall, I trow,
How dear his daughter was to him
3465 (If I die before I do this thing,
Let no man hold it against my name);
For he made me suffer grievous pain.
I feel even now the ancient woe

When I think how he tortured Lupold so."
3470 The noble warriors bedded down
There at Bari in the town.
When morning came they quit the strand.
Then princes hurried through the land.
Lupold journeyed to Milan,
3475 Berchter hastened to Meran.
A doughty youth then did not stay:
Towards Tengeling he made his way.
Wolfrat it was, a hero bold.
Now our story will unfold
3480 How these gentlemen restored
Honorably to their lord
A lady of surpassing worth,
Who to young Pippin then gave birth,
From whom Karl later came to us
3485 And also a maiden most virtuous.
(Saint Gertrude is the one I mean:
At Nivelle her chapel can be seen,
And she helps the sinner willingly
If penitent he prove to be.)
3490 In view of such facts no one may say
That our poem lies in any way.
   The appointed day did soon draw near.
Many a man then donned his gear
In readiness for the great campaign
3495 Which had been vowed in Rother's name.
An ancient man then made his way
Across the land in fine array.
To Bari he came riding
To spread the welcome tiding
3500 That many a lad was coming there.
He rode upon a courser fair.
Upon the shield of the hero bold
Was to be seen a boss of gold.
The shield was made in such a way
3505 That it caught up the light of day
And sent it back with a blinding glare.
He wore a tight-fitting hauberk there.
Down to his belt his beard did hang.
There never lived another man

L. 3486 *Saint Gertrude* — especially honored in the Rhineland; actually the daughter of Pipin of Landen.
L. 3487 *Nivelle* — in Belgium.

3510 Who was deserving of greater praise
      Than the noble Berchter in those days.
      Rother went to greet the lord,
      As with his honor it did accord.
      Likewise did Sir Asprian,
3515 And so did Widolt, the valiant man.
      Then Berchter said: "Ah, noble King,
      Reward me for the news I bring!
      From this time on be of good cheer!
      Many good lads are riding here.
3520 Now take the burghers with you, pray,
      And ride from Bari straight away
      Out onto the lovely strand.
      There you will see a mighty band
      Before the sun sinks in the west.
3525 I have been sent ahead of the rest
      That I may let you know, O King,
      How great an army we do bring."
         Along with Widolt and Asprian
      The mighty Rother then began
3530 To summon the burghers to their side.
      From Bari then they all did ride
      Out onto the lovely strand.
      The whole horizon from there they scanned.
      Then they espied beneath the sky
3535 A mighty army riding by,
      All in armor fully clad.
      Many an undaunted lad
      The faithful Lupold was leading there.
      He held aloft a banner fair.
3540 Whenever the wind tossed its folds about,
      The reddish gold would then flash out,
      So that it seemed to every eye
      As if it were lightning from the sky.
      Then all the burghers to a man
3545 Who had assembled on the sand
      Said: "Gracious God, what's this we see?
      Who can all those people be
      Riding behind that banner fair?"
      Then Berchter said to Rother there:
3550 "My lord, give ear to what I say!
      Your fellow-warriors ride this way.
      The faithful Lupold it must be,
      Bearing that banner so splendidly.
      (His county he does earn today,

3555 So that you may grant it without dismay.)
Most artfully are its colors blent.
Behind it rides a regiment
Of heroes twenty thousand strong
Whom nothing can resist for long.
3560 For your sake I and my sons agree
To lead these men across the sea."
   Then at the side of Lupold's band
There shone in rivalry through the land
Emeralds and sapphires, too.
3565 Of bachelors a mighty crew
Came riding behind a youthful knight
Who carried a banner snowy white.
Wolfrat of Tengeling was his name,
And with him fifty thousand came,
3570 Warriors most deserving,
From honor never swerving.
Silken stuffs and filigree,
The very best embroidery
Which anyone did ever glimpse
3575 In any campaign before or since —
On horses it all was transported there.
In silken mantles passing fair
The lads from Bavaria rode their way.
Never shone the light of day
3580 Upon so many helms, we're told,
Artfully adorned with gold,
As the hero Wolfrat brought with him
To lend support to his noble kin.
(Bavaria still is known, in truth,
3585 As the home of many a dapper youth.)
   As soon as all that doughty band
Had ridden out onto the strand
And pitched their tents beside the sea,
Then Rother came there speedily
3590 And welcomed Lupold, the noble lord,
As with his honor it did accord,
And also Wolfrat, the hero true,
And many another warrior too.
He greeted all of them to a man.
3595 Then said the giant Asprian:
"Alas, King Rother, woe is me!
That I am now compelled to be
Standing here without a band
Of warriors from my native land —

3600 That's because they live so far away.
I am alone to my dismay!"
"Be silent, my lord Asprian!"
Said to him Widolt, the valiant man.
"There in Constantinople Town,
3605 The citadel of great renown,
Not a house-door will there be
Before which you might station me
Where, if someone is found therein,
Such a battle won't begin
3610 That not before the Judgment Day
Could it be stopped in an honorable way."
    The nobles stayed there overnight.
As soon as morning showed its light,
The noble Berchter did not wait:
3615 He took the hand of Lupold straight
And that of the doughty Lupold, too,
And set out thence without ado.
Erwin carried each man's sword
At the behest of his noble lord.
3620 Then the three advised the king
To pick out from the gathering
Thirty thousand valiant men
And send the others home again;
And with his treasure not to spare
3625 But give to all who wished a share.
When they had given their counsel true,
Swiftly Asprian withdrew
And came back with the king's red gold,
As Berchter had bidden the hero bold,
3630 And handed it out to the warriors then:
He helped them to their homes again.
Then Rother led from his domain
Thirty thousand across the main.
Vessels numbering twenty-two
3635 Were loaded for the heroes true.
Then from the port sailed many a son
Whose father to Bari had never come.
    The sails roared loudly in the wind.
Over the water the vessels skimmed
3640 And within the span of six weeks came
Journeying across the main
To Constantinople Town,
The citadel of great renown.
Below the town a mile or more,

3645 Where woods and hills meet by the shore,
There Rother's men began to lead
Onto the land full many a steed
And bring them under the trees so fair,
So that no one became aware
3650 Anywhere in the Greek domain
Just how many a doughty thane
Was standing in the lovely wood
Along with Rother, the hero good.
(His was the old propriety
3655 And the worldly piety
Which every single man today
Towards his master should display:
Then never could the Devil
Put honest men in peril.)
3660   As soon as that intrepid band
Had left the vessels for the land,
They went at once to take their ease
Underneath the lovely trees.
Then did the mighty Rother say
3665 In an extremely prudent way:
"Hear me, vassals and kinsmen mine!
I now shall go to Constantine
In the disguise of a wayfaring man
Who must beg for his food from land to land.
3670 So may I learn what's going on."
The youthful Wolfrat said thereon
(He was the lord of Tengeling):
"Do not go alone, O King!
Berchter is a prudent knight
3675 And often has advised you right.
And if, my lord, you would maintain
The honor due your noble name,
The faithful Lupold you'll also ask
To help you carry out this task.
3680 Now take this excellent horn of mine:
For all of us it shall be a sign.
The Greeks, in truth, are very clever;
And if they should learn of your endeavor,
Then you'll be seized by Constantine's men."
3685 "Verily", said Asprian then,
"As soon as we hear you blow your horn,
The citadel we'll swiftly storm.
No matter how large the town may be,
I swear by all that's dear to me

3690 That before whatever street I stand
And with me Widolt, the valiant man,
That will become the narrowest road
Along which anyone ever strode!"
    The heroes then did not delay:
3695 They slipped into pilgrims' clothes straightway.
The worthy Berchter of Meran
Along with Lupold, the faithful man,
Went at the side of the mighty king
And left behind the gathering.
3700   Then towards them rode a warrior good
Who'd been watching from the edge of the wood.
The mighty Rother in disguise
Greeted him in courteous wise
And asked the gentleman to say
3705 Whether any news had come his way.
"In me you see a wretched man
Who must beg for his food from land to land.
Now tell me, dear sir, something new!
A needy pilgrim is asking you
3710 Who has to cover many a mile
Suffering sorely all the while.
And so the poor man in his need
Must often to the court proceed.
There one asks the wayfaring man
3715 To tell whatever news he can.
For God's sake tell some news to me!
Well rewarded you will be."
    The worthy hero replied thereto:
"Plenty of news I have for you.
3720 Here in Constantinople Town,
The citadel of great renown,
A very noble exile dwelled,
For splendid manners unexcelled.
(To this I always can attest,
3725 For he gave me nothing but the best.)
The princes all did love the youth.
He gave to them more gold, in truth,
Than ever before fell to the share
Of anybody anywhere.
3730 The doors of his court stood open wide
To let the poor and the rich inside.
They soon found in the hero true
A father and a mother, too.
His whole ambition was but to give.

3735 He did not care at all to live
With any kind of surfeit.
He waged a war against it.
Both night and day he brought it lower.
If one asked for a thousand pounds or more,
3740 He gave it away as easily
As if two pennies it might be.
Now tarry, sir, and I shan't fail
To let you hear the rest of my tale."
    Rother thought it lots of fun
3745 To hear what he himself had done.
The warrior went on straightway:
"About this lord I've more to say!
We loved him for his gentle ways.
A man deserving of greater praise
3750 Because of his goodness was never seen
Anywhere on earth, I ween.
I don't know of anyone at all
Who would be able to recall
All of the hero's excellent deeds.
3755 He attended to the exiles' needs.
The wretched lads were bathed and dressed
And served at the table at his behest.
Whatever was his he gave to them there.
He didn't care who took his share.
3760 He led so many a doughty youth
That under the heavens, in very truth,
No exiled man was able to boast
Of having gathered a greater host.
He proved his valor for all time
3765 By saving the mighty Constantine
When he was in a dangerous spot.
He captured the Emperor Ymelot,
A terrible paynim, so they say,
Who received the homage every day
3770 Of princes two-and-seventy strong
From the land of Egyptian Babylon.
Joyfully our army then
Began to journey home again.
The king then sent the valiant man
3775 Ahead as an envoy to our land
That he might tell to the ladies fair
All that he had accomplished there.
Now here in Constantinople Town,
The citadel of great renown,

3780 There was residing a maiden fair
With whom no other could compare.
For her he suffered grievous dole
And with decorum achieved his goal
So that the maiden did not fear
3785 To run with him away from here
Before the army came back home.
He took her in payment for his own
And traveled westward over the sea.
The King of Rome he proved to be,
3790 Rother, a man of noble mind
And to all of us extremely kind.
Now, good pilgrim, you shall be told
How one paid back the hero bold."
 Rother wished to go from there.
3795 Then said to him the hero fair:
"Tarry a moment, pilgrim, do!
Important news I have for you.
When Constantine came back one day,
The paynim managed to run away.
3800 The king dispatched some envoys then
To win his daughter back again.
They stole her from Rother cleverly
And brought her back across the sea.
Then Ymelot, the paynim lord,
3805 Came riding with a mighty horde
Hither to this Grecian land,
And burned and pillaged on every hand,
And captured the Emperor Constantine,
That very hateful lord of mine.
3810 Then Constantine redeemed his life
By handing over Rother's wife
To that king so fierce to look upon
From the land of Egyptian Babylon.
Wedded to his son she'll be,
3815 As you this very night can see.
Thirty kings have settled down
At Constantinople in the town
Together with an army strong
From the land of Egyptian Babylon.
3820 Rother's wife is among them there
And keeps chastising her body fair
On account of her very grievous plight.
Now may our Savior in His might
Send Asprian to us anon

3825 Before this day has passed and gone."
To this the nobles said "Amen!
Upon God's grace it does depend."
Swiftly then the hero good
Galloped off into the wood,
3830 Wringing his hands as he rode his way
And sorely weeping in his dismay.
In such wise did that worthy knight
Bewail the damsel's grievous plight.
   Into the city Rother hied.
3835 Berchter went at his master's side
And warned him not to be too bold.
The mighty Constantine, we're told,
Along with many another lord
Was seated at a festive board
3840 Within a hall most fair to see.
Great was the noise of revelry
In front of the princes thirty strong
From the land of Egyptian Babylon.
Then Rother crept with sly design
3845 To the table of King Constantine.
Beside the king sat Ymelot's son
(His name was Basilistium).
Next to him sat Rother's mate
And did not cease to bewail her fate.
3850   Then said the mighty Constantine:
"Stop your weeping, daughter mine!
I had a dream last night of you
(You can believe that I speak true)
How a falcon flew here to our strand
3855 All the way from the Roman land
And carried you back across the sea."
   Rother then crept stealthily
Under the table with his men,
So that no one was aware of them.
3860 And so he could overhear everything
That the guests were speaking with the king.
   The princes then began to boast
About the strength of the paynim host.
"If Rother should show up," said they,
3865 "We'd see that he was drowned straightway
Or otherwise slain shamefully —
How angry then would Widolt be!"
To them the queen replied: "I vow
That if our Lord were to send him now

3870 Here among you heroes true,
He would belabor some of you
So that even after a sevennight
The pain would not have vanished quite."
　　Rother moved closer without being seen
3875 Upon the footstool of the queen.
Then he took a golden ring with care
And passed it to his lady fair.
(Letters were engraved therein
Which spelled the name of the mighty king.)
3880 As soon as the lady became aware
That her mighty lord was hiding there,
Then she began to smile anon
And told her mother thereupon
That Rother had, without any doubt,
3885 Come from Bari to help them out.
　　By Constantine the smile was seen.
Now hear how he addressed the queen:
"Blessings on you, daughter dear!
Now my heart is filled with cheer."
3890 The splendid dame replied thereto:
"In very truth, I now must rue
That with you I was ever wroth.
'Tis the very last time, upon my oath!"
Ymelot said thereupon:
3895 "Lady, you need not put on.
It's my belief that your smiling now
Will cause us heartfelt grief somehow.
When it is finished there will be
Wringing of hands, in all verity.
3900 Be on your guard now one and all!
Somewhere here inside the hall
The hateful envoys tarry
Of Rother, King of Bari.
If anyone doubts what I have said,
3905 To him I'm ready to give my head!"
　　Thereupon said Ymelot's son
(His name was Basilistium):
"Just now I saw a handsome ring
Which by your daughter was slipped, O King,
3910 Into the hand of the ancient queen.
Somewhere in the hall, I ween,
The mighty King of Rome does hide,
Though I don't know how he got inside.
You can depend on what I say!"

3915 Then Constantine said right away:
"Before the door I shall command
Twelve of my men to take their stand
So that they may properly recognize
If here among us are any spies.
3920 Should Rother now be hiding here,
We'll quickly find him, never fear!
But if he were to show his face,
It surely would bring less disgrace
Upon the mighty king, I vow,
3925 Than if we had to search for him now
As though he were a runaway thief.
It doesn't become him in the least
That he refuses to appear,
Even though we know that he is here."
3930   Rother pondered secretly
What his conduct now should be.
To him the Duke of Meran said:
"Let each of us now show his head
In honor of the Heavenly King
3935 And all His mighty following,
So that of His benevolence
He'll quickly come to our defence
Against the heathens in this hour.
In token of His mighty power
3940 He bade that Moses undertake
By way of the Red Sea his escape
With the children of Israel.
Not one of them was forced to dwell
Upon that awful water's ground.
3945 Thus are good and evil bound
By our Heavenly Father still,
Even though one resist His will.
Provided we have always been
Wholly pure and free from sin
3950 In our Heavenly Father's sight,
He'll not forsake us in our plight.
Now I swear by Saint Aegidius' name
That here no longer will I remain!"
In this wise Berchter spoke to them.
3955 From underneath the table then
Slyly crept the gentlemen.
The noble Rother walked ahead.
"Verily, I am here," he said.
"Whoso desires may look on me!"

3960 Then all the princes equally
Threatened to slay him right away —
For which some later had to pay.
   Then said the Emperor Ymelot's son
(His name was Basilistium):
3965 "Rother, were it up to me,
I'd have you thrown into the sea.
'Twas you who took my father alive—
Because of which you shan't survive!
Your life you must prepare to lose,
3970 Howsoever you may choose."
   "Upon my word", said Constantine,
"A shameful death would suit him fine!"
To this the mighty king did say
In an extremely clever way:
3975 "Even though you freed me now,
I still could not survive, I vow.
Do you see those mountains over there,
Standing in front of that forest fair?
That is where I wish to hang.
3980 Your followers you should command
To give you all the help you need —
You yourself shall do the deed.
In my domain it is only right,"
Went on to say the honest knight,
3985 "That whatsoever a prince befall,
Another prince must see it all.
Here is a mighty company,
Thirty princes, verily!
Thither with you they shall come
3990 And with me they will have their fun;
And so you will enhance your name.
Then Ymelot's men will all proclaim
How you avenged yourself on me."
The lord spoke very cleverly!
3995 Close by the spot where he would hang
Was lying his intrepid band.
He had picked out the very spot
To which Sir Asprian had got.
   Ymelot bade the princes strong
4000 From the land of Egyptian Babylon
To seize King Rother straight away:
He wished to hang him without delay.
"In truth," said Constantine, "I should like
To be of assistance if I might,

4005 So that he doesn't escape from us.
　　… … … … … … … … … … … … …
That ancient fellow with the beard
Is by the people greatly feared
When through the land he leads his men.
Now that we have all three of them,
4010 We probably shan't have to fear
Lest the Roman folk should ever hear
Whither their mighty king did wend
Or how he happened to meet his end."
　　The awful moment had come round.
4015 Rother's hands were quickly bound
(That was the work of Ymelot's men).
How bitterly the young queen then
Filled the air with her complaint.
From grief she fell into a faint.
4020 How very great was her travail!
Then there began to weep and wail
The ladies fair on every side:
Their flowing tears they could not hide.
No need was there for one to ask.
4025 Everybody was aghast
At the noble Rother's plight.
(Later the good Lord in His might
Helped Count Arnold rescue him
From Ymelot, the terrible king.)
4030 　　The news that Rother was to hang
Quickly spread from man to man
In Constantinople Town,
The citadel of great renown,
Till it came to the ears of the heroes fair
4035 Who from many a land had gathered there.
They all began to weep full sore
As they ran down towards the shore.
They raised their voices in a shout.
"Amighty God," they all cried out,
4040 "How could You let it come about
That fettered now that man should be
Who saved us all from misery?"
　　A nobleman was living well
On the thousand pounds, so we hear tell,
4045 Which Rother had given him for his share.
Seven hundred warriors fair

　L. 4005 A line is missing here.

Paid him service in the town:
To him in fealty they were bound.
Arnold was his name, we're told,
4050 And he had plenty of silver and gold,
Which he took pleasure in giving away.
Twelve hundred men in full array
He led towards the shouting then,
And ordered all his noble men
4055 To liberate with their own hands
The mighty Rother from his bands.
"The lord is standing fettered there.
If he should hang today, I swear
That we will never know any peace.
4060 Nor will the Romans ever cease
From mourning the loss of the hero true.
Never will any one of you
Hear of a man who was his peer.
Today we should repay him here
4065 For having deigned to set us free
From lives of direst misery.
Up, good lads, and don't delay!
Put your trust in God this day
And come to the aid of the noble lord.
4070 Heaven will be your reward."
Thus spoke Arnold, a worthy knight.
"Truly, we defend God's right.
If anyone today is slain,
Eternal bliss his soul will gain.
4075 Let's kill these paynims one and all!
May Saint Aegidius recall
And Saint John the Baptist, too,
That never lived a king more true
Than the noble Rother anywhere —
4080 To the truth of which I'm ready to swear!"
   Many a hero unafraid
In coat of mail was soon arrayed.
Truly, they were a splendid sight!
Five thousand warriors well-bedight
4085 Were ready to perish in the fray
If Rother might be saved that day.
   Forth from Constantinople Town,
The citadel of great renown,
Thirty princes marched along,

L. 4076 *Aegidius* — a saint much revered in the Rhineland.

4090 Followed by a mighty throng.
At their head went Basilistium
(He was the Emperor Ymelot's son)
And led King Rother along the way:
He wished to see him hang that day.
4095 Then there was raised a mighty cry
As they led the hero forth to die.
To the gallows-place there went along
Cumans a hundred thousand strong,
And as many of the paynim horde.
4100 How deeply that did grieve the lord!
Count Arnold showed no sign of fear.
He bound a reliquary to his spear
Which in the church he had obtained.
Then calling on our Savior's name
4105 He led his followers from the town.
How eager was he to reach open ground!
Fighting-men five thousand strong
In shining armor he led along.
    When Ymelot espied this host,
4110 This is the way he began to boast:
"Ha! take a look at those warriors there!
They thought to give us all a scare.
I'll wreak my wrath on every one.
Alive from here not one shall come!"
4115   The paynim army soon drew nigh
To the spot where Rother was to die.
On every side they raised a din.
"Now build the gallows high for him!"
This moved the heroes to the core.
4120 Many of them wept much more
Than they had ever done before.
Rother's need was very sore!
The valiant Arnold then began
To call on many an exiled man.
4125 "Worthy lads, give ear, I pray,
To what we're fighting for today.
Two rewards we have in sight:
All the more gladly should we fight!
The first reward is fair indeed:
4130 The Kingdom of Heaven will be our meed.
If any of you shall die today,

  L. 4098 *Cumans* — an Asiatic nomadic people which invaded Europe around 1045; known among the Slavs as Polovtsi.

           His soul will be released straightway
           To another life of lasting bliss.
           What gift was ever better than this?"
     4135 Now hear about the second reward!
           If you shall save our faithful lord,
           He'll take you with him overseas
           And assure you of a life of ease."
           His eyes began to dim with grief.
     4140 Strengthened by the true belief,
           They fell upon the paynims then
           And slew a mighty host of them.
              The armor of the paynim throng
           Proved to be exceeding strong:
     4145 The suits they wore were made of horn.
           On high the relic then was borne
           Before the eyes of the heroes bold.
           Into the thick of the fray they rode.
           The relic was always in the van.
     4150 In God confided every man.
           So fiercely did the heroes fight
           That nothing could withstand their might.
           The infidels were driven back
           Before the force of their attack.
     4155   From the gallows-place there then withdrew
           The paynims and the Cumans, too.
           Verily, they were sore bestead!
           Many a hero lay there dead.
           Then Arnold did not hesitate:
     4160 He gave from his hand his standard straight
           And drew a sword (its name was Mal).
           Never had any steel at all
           Been made so rigid or so hard
           That it wasn't able to split apart.
     4165 Because of this he was able to slay
           Six of the princes right away.
           To whomsoever else he came
           The hero quickly did the same,
           Until he had rescued the noble man
     4170 Together with Berchter of Meran
           And also Lupold, a hero fair,
           Whom they had wanted to string up there.
           If on our story we can rely,
           No one could keep on them an eye.
     4175 Those who wanted to wreak them woe
           Said that God had willed it so.

As soon as Rother became aware
That Arnold was standing beside him there,
He cried out to the valiant knight
4180 In a manner that beseemed him quite:
"Cut asunder now these bands,
Doughty warrior, from my hands,
And when upon my horn I blow
Many more will be laid low
4185 Than have been up to now, I swear!
To us will Asprian soon repair."
As soon as the warriors heard his name,
How happy all of them became!
Eager were they for the fray.
4190 Not a thought did they give to running away.
Truly, they were a valiant band!
   At that time there were upon the strand
Seven heathen princes still,
With eighty thousand to do their will.
4195 Loudly a horn resounded then
Over the mountain and the glen.
It had been blown by Rother's man,
The faithful Lupold of Milan.
Then in a loud voice Asprian said:
4200 "God knows, my master is sore bestead!
Wolfrat, don your armor straight:
I think your cousin's need is great.
Of Rother I shan't speak at all;
But if Sir Lupold were to fall,
4205 His loss we'd never cease to rue.
No hero ever was more true."
   Widolt hurried from the wood
Just as swiftly as he could.
How his hauberk gave a clang
4210 Whenever over a bush he sprang!
After him came Asprian.
The twelve ferocious giants ran
Over paths both good and bad.
Accompanied by many a lad,
4215 Wolfrat of Tengeling came with speed:
A splendid army he did lead
Forth from the middle of the wood.
To Rother were pledged the heroes good.
Many a lad in full array
4220 Hurried there along the way.
   On every side could be heard the din.

From the gallows then they rescued him
And listened to how the earth did shake.
Two terrible giants full of hate
4225 Were coming thither on the run.
Of them Asprian was one.
The other was Widolt, a hero bold.
(Across the land shone forth the gold
Which adorned the margin of his shield.)
4230 From Ymelot was not concealed
What Rother had in mind for them.
How gladly would he have run off then!
Many a paynim started running.
Asprian set the wind a-humming.
4235 Towards him Rother made his way.
"Listen, bold hero, to what I say!
The giants mustn't harm a hair
Of those who are standing with Lupold there.
Those gentlemen are the very same
4240 Who helped me to avoid great shame.
In fetters I was forced to stand.
Then I was just about to be hanged
By those princes so fierce to look upon
From the land of Egyptian Babylon.
4245 Now I don't care how they're made to pay.
I shan't interfere in any way!"
Then Grimme cried for all to hear:
"They'll never get away from here!"
   The giants ran onto the battle-ground.
4250 From the host there rose a mighty sound.
Asprian began to slay
Whosoever crossed his way.
By Widolt not a word was spoken
Until to bits his club was broken.
4255 The savage fellow drew thereon
A club most awful to look upon.
Into shreds were cut the horses then
Which were lying on the dying men.
From many a wound the blood did gush
4260 When the valiant Wolfrat with a rush
Hurried into the midst of the fight
Along with many another knight.
The doughty lads performed that day
Such deeds of daring in the fray
4265 As will forever enjoy renown,
Because the facts have been written down

Concerning all that company
Who almost had been forced to flee.
　The seven princes turned away
4270 From the center of the fray.
Truly, they were terrified!
At one of them did Erwin ride.
He struck the devilish man a blow
From his shoulder down to the saddle-bow
4275 All the way through his horny attire.
Thus did the hero avenge his sire.
Five of them they hanged straightway.
How dearly were they made to pay!
The heathen slaughter then began.
4280 Upon the field lay many a man.
Whenever one cried out in pain,
Widolt rushed at him amain
And dealt him such a vicious kick
That he never did get over it.
4285 They had good reason to feel dismay
And to await the Judgment Day,
Because not one did the giant spare.
Ymelot, who had led them there,
Was bidden then to go his way
4290 And set out thence without delay,
So that at home he might proclaim
By whom his followers had been slain.
　A hundred minstrels, so we're told,
Had come there with the paynims bold.
4295 The hero Grimme had them bound
And stretched full-length upon the ground.
A thorough switching they got that day;
For Ymelot they were made to pay.
Then one of the minstrels managed to flee
4300 Who had fled from Widolt previously.
To Constantine he came apace,
As fast as he was able to race.
Then all the princes questioned him
About the reason for the din
4305 Which they heard coming from the field.
"Important news shall be revealed!
The prisoner has gotten clear.
With an army they are riding here.
Whoever would not hang today
4310 Had better not stay here, I say!
The hero Widolt is giving away

Over yonder food and pay
To many an unbelieving wretch.
Upon the ground I was made to stretch.
4315 Then I was lashed with whips and shorn.
My life I almost had forsworn!
But this I truly can report:
For bruises of the finest sort
Widolt's club can't be outdone.
4320 They've hanged Prince Basilistium.
They're not content to chop off a foot;
They help you out of this life, to boot.
Now the Devil is making a fool of me!
Why do I show such courtesy
4325 And stand here talking so long with you?
Question some other fellow, do!
Whosoever is seized today
Forevermore will have to pay!"
Quickly then they all took flight.
4330 Brooding over his grievous plight
Sat Constantine, the mighty king.
How shameful all this was to him!
   Our story now goes on to say
How the lads from Rome began straightway
4335 To pull back all their forces
And catch once more their horses.
Then had the wrath of Wolfrat made
Bloody traces with his blade,
Deep incisions with his spear,
4340 Cloven through the helmet sheer
Of many a sorely wounded man.
By means of his undaunted hand
The hero sent upon his way
Many a worthy lad that day
4345 To an unpleasant reckoning.
(He was the lord of Tengeling,
And came from an illustrious clan —
A rich yet not a haughty man,
And of a very prudent mind;
4350 And so to his family he left behind
The right to bear a princely name
As long as this world does remain.)
   In front of Arnold took his stand
The worthy Berchter of Meran.
4355 Beside the latter Wolfrat stood,
Who has deserved all that is good,

And Erwin, who excelled always
Wherever one could earn great praise
And proved himself untiringly.
4360 (Indeed, no one knew better than he
How to advise an honest knight
So that his business went just right
Even to the end of his days —
One had good reason to sing his praise!)
4365 After them a wise man came
(Lupold of Milan was his name)
Who never had in his domain
Done aught to cause him any shame.
Truly, he was a well-bred knight
4370 And never boasted of his might.
A proper course he always steered.
By honest lads he had been reared
Till he was knighted with the sword.
Rother then with many a lord
4375 In Arnold's presence swore an oath
That, should the hero not be loath,
To their assistance he could look
In whatsoever he undertook.
Henceforth he lived without a care.
4380 This was the reward of the hero fair
For having given proof that day
Of his great valor in the fray.
(Just so will that man receive his meed
Who accomplishes some valiant deed.)
4385   Asprian pondered in his mind
What they should do with Constantine.
Said Grimme: "He may not survive!
In the city he must burn alive.
Now let us take his daughter dear,
4390 For whom we made this journey here,
And set the town on fire straight.
Let Widolt stand before the gate.
If anyone tries to leave that way,
How dearly he will make him pay!
4395 But if he should manage to escape,
No further action will we take."
"Upon my oath", said Asprian,
"You're going to let the city stand.
Seven apostles full of grace
4400 Once found here a resting-place,
As did that very virtuous dame

From whom the Emperor Constantine came —
Helen, who the cross did find
On which the Lord redeemed mankind.
4405 When He ascended from the grave,
Redemption to all those He gave
Whose downfall Adam brought about
Because he would not do without
That against which God had warned.
4410 He by whom we all were formed
Has all the world in His command.
Both the forest and the strand
He created and the sea
In His tremendous majesty.
4415 Whosoever serves the Lord
Can be assured of his reward.
Never will he go astray
Nor will his handiwork pass away
From eternity to eternity.
4420 And so it would seem good to me,"
Declared the giant Asprian,
"If you spared that ancient gentleman."
   In the fear of God did Widolt stand.
And so henceforth throughout the land
4425 He was a friend of the heroes proud.
"Holy God!" he cried aloud,
"What would You have of me poor wight,
Seeing that wisdom I'm lacking quite?
As soon as my body is no more,
4430 What then lies for my soul in store?
Alas, that I was ever bred!
The Devil put it into my head
That I most miserable clown
Wanted to burn the city down.
4435 O Lord, I have sinned badly!
And yet would I right gladly
Receive Your grace before I die.
Very much afraid am I
That just as it was with my birth,
4440 So You will take me from this earth
With all my sins condemning me.
The fiery pit You did decree
For every wicked sinner here.
How very much do I revere
4445 The good Saint Michael there on high:
In him the soul has an ally.

'Twas he who brought the Devil low.
He gave him such a mighty blow
That he fell into eternal flame.
4450 Because his pride he could not tame,
He was no longer allowed to be
One of that heavenly company."
   The giants then did not delay:
To a man they threw their clubs away.
4455 For the sake of the Eternal Christ,
Who had given them the gift of life,
They did not harm the famous town —
Else they would surely have burned it down.
   Rother bade that one should bring
4460 The faithful Lupold there to him.
He summoned the mighty Berchter too,
Who always gave him counsel true.
"O King", the latter then did say,
"Give heed to God and your soul today
4465 That honor may be yours alway.
Do not allow the town to fall.
Should Constantine be harmed at all,
Guilty of that we all shall be
And must be damned eternally.
4470 I tell you truly, master dear,
That Constantine I do revere.
Now may this profit the mighty king!
God Who fashioned everything
Punishes that man indeed
4475 Who breaks the limits He has decreed,
For then he leaves the proper way.
Our Savior does truly say
That whoever is bound by love to him
Must be at all times free from sin.
4480 Now, dear sir, I beg of you:
Send for your wife without more ado!"
   To this the mighty king did say
In an extremely prudent way:
"Since my father ceased to be
4485 And you were put in charge of me,
You have looked after my good name
With the utmost devotion, worthy thane.
You guarded me both night and day
So that no harm did come my way;
4490 And you brought me up like your own son.
(Most Christianly was all this done!)

And you taught me too that honest knights
Should never be injured in their rights.
Now may Almighty God above,
4495 In token of His lasting love,
Reward you for your service true.
I shall not cease to mourn for you
If I survive you, worthy thane —
Nothing could cause me greater pain!"
4500   These words King Rother fully meant.
To flatter was not his intent.
At that time every hero good
Avoided sin as best he could
And only said what was in his mind
4505 About the rest of humankind —
Lest he should have to suffer shame.
The princes then were free from blame.
They dwelled in the kingdom, so we hear,
And faithfully served their master dear.
4510   Very much afraid meantime
Was the mighty Constantine.
Unto the queen he then did cry:
"Ah, dear wife, how much do I
Regret that into this world I came —
4515 By Rother's men I shall be slain!
What folly was I guilty of
... ...
That ever I snatched his wife away!
For that I now shall dearly pay.
Besides, there was no reason to;
4520 He always rendered service true.
And yet I wickedly essayed
To have that gentleman repayed
By letting him hang this very day.
It often happens, people say,
4525 That what a man has one time done
He meets on all sides later on.
'Twas I myself who dug this pit.
Now I shall have to lie in it
(As I deserve for my behavior)
4530 Unless I'm saved by Christ our Savior
And by His gracious mother too.
Now take my daughter along with you
And go forth with her from the town

  L. 4516 A line is missing here.

And before the gentleman kneel down
4535 And for the Lord's sake plead with him
To reflect upon the plight I'm in
And not deprive me of my life.
And tell him further, gracious wife,
That here in the city I shall dwell,
4540 So that till Doomsday one will tell
How much was accomplished by the man
When Rother did not let him hang."
  Now hear the answer the good queen made!
"O Constantine, why be afraid?
4545 Those princes can surely be counted on
From the land of Egyptian Babylon
To help you hang the mighty king.
Perhaps you still can capture him.
'Tis pride has been your downfall!
4550 You wouldn't listen to me at all.
You treated God with the utmost scorn,
At Whose command we all were born,
And after the Devil you chose to go,
By whom in the end you've been brought low.
4555 With God you would have been better off.
The Devil will fling you into his trough
Where you and all your pals in sin
Will be able neither to wade nor swim.
From all this you can understand
4560 That there is nothing that a man
Ought to avoid on every side
More than the accursed pride,
By which the Devil has brought it about
That he has never yet run out
4565 Of "Oh me!" and "Ah me!"
And every kind of misery —
Of which he never has a lack;
And he'll give you some if you follow his track."
  Constantine considered how
4570 He could manage it somehow
That he'd be spared by Rother's men.
This seemed to him the best plan then:
He bade his daughter visit him there,
Clad in raiment passing fair.
4575 Then women and maidens began straightway
To dress themselves in their finest array.
They put on mantles, so we're told,
Which had been trimmed with cloth of gold

And adorned with precious jewelry,
4580 Set in gold most skilfully.
To Constantine then did repair
Eighty ladies passing fair.
Decorously they walked along.
A golden crown from each one shone.
4585   To the Hippodrome one began to lead
Many a palfrey and many a steed.
Then one could hear the tinkling tones
Of dainty pearls against precious stones
Which adorned the horses' breast-straps.
4590 The saddles were in velvet wraps
Which shone forth with a greenish hue —
In case our story tells us true.
Upon a silken covering
Was seated the daughter of the king.
4595 Constantine without his men
Rode in the midst of the ladies then.
Next to him the queen did ride;
His daughter was on his other side.
A sapphire then sent forth its light
4600 (Wherever it shone 'twas never night)
From the crown upon the maiden's hair.
Together with his daughter fair
And eighty damsels in fine array
The Emperor rode on his way
4605 From Constantinople Town
To where King Rother held the ground.
    The sound of the bridles filled the air
As from the town the ladies fair
4610 Hurried forth in friendly strife.
Across the land King Rother's wife
Shone brighter than any other dame —
Just like a sapphire all aflame.
When Erwin saw them drawing nigh,
4615 Then to his master he did cry:
"Your hateful father-in-law I see!
Receive him with propriety.
Think of the honored ways of yore—
How noblemen would heretofore
4620 Forgive an injury in God's name.
Now do not put the world to shame
By the way you treat the honest knight.
Truly, it would not be right,
Seeing that the mighty lord

4625 Comes riding here of his own accord,
If you were to rob him of his life.
He is bringing you the most beautiful wife!"
Said Asprian: "'Twere well enough
If he were given a proper cuff!"
4630 Then did the mighty Berchter say
In an extremely fitting way:
"O noble Asprian, speak not so!
Courtesy we all must show,
Now that he comes in the midst of these wives.
4635 And though he should have taken the lives
Of all my children, still I swear
That we ought to honor these ladies fair
By sparing the life of the mighty king —
Else great misfortune it will bring.
4640 When a man comes seeking clemency,
It is only right to hear his plea."
Then did the mighty Rother say
In an extremely proper way:
"Soldiers from the Roman land,
4645 Hearken now to my command!
Welcome Constantine the Great
In courteous fashion for my sake."
Then Berchter quickly rose from there
And went to meet the lady fair.
4650 Lupold and Erwin did the same:
They hurried forward to greet the dame.
Rother kissed his lovely wife
(She was as dear to him as his life).
He also kissed the ancient queen
4655 And welcomed her with courteous mien.
The valiant Wolfrat went betime
And took the hand of Constantine.
As soon as Widolt caught sight of him,
His face became exceeding grim.
4660 He fell to the ground and started to bite
His club with so much appetite
That flames shot forth into the sky.
What terrible looks could one espy
Upon the face of the valiant man!
4665 Near him no one dared to stand
Unless he spoke nice words to him.
He raised up there a greater din
Than hitherto he had ever made,
Whatever may have been his trade.

4670 How rightly had the queen espied
That Widolt couldn't be pacified.
To Constantine she turned her head
And in most courteous fashion said:
"Closer to Rother you should stand!
4675 Yonder is Sir Asprian's man;
His anger no one can allay.
Supposing that this very day
You gave up your accustomed ways.
How with his club that fellow plays,
4680 So that from it the flames do fly
Higher and higher into the sky!
If it weren't for the king's good name,
Never would you see again
Either your people or your land:
4685 You would be slain by that devil's hand.
If from his chains he break away,
You will not see another day!"
    The queen took the hand of her daughter fair
(She was a lady beyond compare).
4690 "Rother, master of my life,
I bring you here your lawful wife.
Take command again of her
As you think proper, gracious sir.
May God bestow His grace on you
4695 And on all these other nobles, too,
For many an honor paid to me.
You, Duke Berchter, are known to be
A hero most deserving,
In loyalty unswerving,
4700 And you serve our Lord untiringly.
Blessed must your mother be
That ever she gave birth to you!
You are an upright man and true.
Today you've shown your breeding
4705 By hearkening to our pleading
And allowing Constantine to go free,
Though he treated you so grievously."
(She spoke about the honest knight
In a manner that he merited quite.
4710 Vengefulness he had always spurned,
As from our story you have learned.)
    Then did the Emperor Constantine say:
"Rother, my dear lord, I pray
That you will have Arnold brought to us.

4715 To him I would be generous
Because of the valor with which he fought,
So that he may never lack for aught.
He hastened to rescue you, hero bold."
Then he was given a crown of gold
4720 And the right to govern his own domain:
The King of Greece he then became.
Then noblemen five thousand strong
Who at his bidding had marched along
From Constantinople so fair to see
4725 Pledged to him their fealty.
Merrily then he rode away
To his domain that very day.
There one paid him great respect,
Which the worthy hero kept
4730 Until the very day he died.
In this way he was satisfied.
If some young man were to ponder this,
It surely would not come amiss,
For if he zealously serve his lord,
4735 He can be certain of his reward.

    The noblemen withdrew from there.
To Greece Count Arnold did repair.
The lovely queen then walked around
The troops assembled on that ground
4740 And kissed each one of Rother's men:
To God she commended all of them.
The valiant Wolfrat, so we're told,
With eighty thousand heroes bold
Hurried then to board a ship
4745 Which had been laden for the trip.
It brought the noble Rother home
With his fair wife across the foam.
Then into the ship the warriors pressed:
This was at Asprian's behest.
4750 Then to their homeland did repair
That company of nobles fair.
Then Constantine began to ride
Wit his good lady at his side
Back to Constantinople Town,
4755 The citadel of great renown.
His daughter's loss gave him no pain.
He now rejoiced in Rother's fame.

    The ships sailed smoothly over the sea.
Rother and his company

4760	Journeyed on across the foam
	And came again to the soil of Rome.
	At Bari they landed on the strand.
	Then horses and raiment were brought on land
	And all that the ships contained of worth.
4765	To Pippin then the queen gave birth
	On that very day and not before
	When they set foot upon the shore.
	Then Lupold did not hesitate:
	He hurried to King Rother straight
4770	And said "Rejoice, O worthy King!
	Pleasant tidings I do bring!
	What you are about to hear is true:
	Your wife has borne a son to you!"
	Then Rother jumped up full of glee.
4775	"O God, how thankful must I be
	For the grace which You have deigned to show
	To this poor sinner here below!
	Now it's clear that he who cleaves to You
	Will never have any cause to rue
4780	Having lost the Realm Divine:
	You will sustain him all the time."
	As soon as the chaplains heard this news,
	Then not a minute did they lose:
	They baptized at once the little tot.
4785	Pippin was the name it got.
	Then many a nurse was seen to come
	Into the castle on the run:
	They saw that the child was carefully bred.
	Later with Bertha he was wed.
4790	(She was a lady of notable worth,
	Who later on to Karl gave birth.)
	In view of such facts it would be wrong
	To compare this with some other song,
	Because it tells only what is so —
4795	Whence for it the truth does flow.
	Upon his throne sat the mighty king.
	Gathered there in front of him
	Could be seen a mighty crowd.
	Thereupon the heroes proud
4800	Began to think of traveling home,
	Because each one of them had known
	During the course of the campaign
	Many a moment of grievous pain.
	Then every man began to pray

4805 That Rother would not say them nay
But would allow them to go their way.
The king knelt down before his men
And in God's name entreated them:
"Vassals and kinsmen, say not so!
4810 Do not think so soon to go!
Bide a while for Jesus' sake
Till recompense I'm able to make —
Else it would be the greatest shame
That to a mortal ever came
4815 Here upon this earth, I trow."
Then many a good lad answered so:
"God Almighty knows, my lord,
You've given us our just reward."
Then Asprian the giant cried:
4820 "Here in this land we must abide!
Never shall I journey hence
Until the gracious king consents."
    The mighty Rother rewarded then
Every one of his doughty men,
4825 Just as honor does still demand.
He gave away the English land
To Grimme (he was a giant bold);
There he resided, so we're told,
In high esteem for many a day.
4830 To Asprian he gave away
Reims and the land that belonged thereto:
He had proved himself a vassal true.
The wealthy Scottish realm he gave
Unto the other ten giants brave.
4835 Brabant and Lothringia,
The Netherland and Frisia
Four noblemen received in fee
Who had sailed with him across the sea
In furtherance of his pursuit.
4840 (Verily, each one was a duke!)
He enriched them all with property.
Faithful had they proved to be.
    Rother sat with bounteous hand
And freely parceled out his land.
4845 Many a man was enriched by him.
Spain he gave to Erwin.
Saxony and Thuringia,
The Pleissnerland and Sorbia
He awarded to ten counts that day

4850 Who on his behalf had sailed away
With the faithful Lupold across the sea:
He rewarded them most generously.
Whoever had served him loyally
He rewarded there most royally.
4855 His treasure no one wished to share,
Nor did he offer his coursers fair.
Whosoever had proved his worth
Was paid by him with the broad earth.
   Now the writer will not fail
4860 To go on telling you his tale.
It gives much pleasure to honest folk.
To the good-for-nothing it's but a joke:
Worthy deeds they have never done,
And they don't believe them of anyone.
4865   Deep in thought sat the hero good
And gave away whatever he could.
Then he did summon there to him
The worthy lord of Tengeling,
And invested him with Austria,
4870 Poland and Bohemia:
All this he was right glad to give
So that the more worthily he might live.
There never dwelled beside the sea
A noble of such high degree
4875 Either before or since that day.
Over the whole world he held sway.
Rich in land was he indeed,
And was of that true princes' breed
Who all have lived in such a way
4880 That no one ever was heard to say
That they had been false to anyone.
To a worthy end they all did come.
   Carefully did the noble lord
Consider whom he should reward.
4885 He summoned to him Sir Lupold then
There in the sight of all his men
And paid to the youthful knight his thanks
By making him ruler of the Franks.
To Berchter then he gave in fee
4890 Apulia and Sicily,
So that the holdings were very wide
Across which Berchter had to ride
Many a winter fully geared.
Down the ancient warrior's beard

4895 The raindrops very often ran.
Truly, he was a dauntless man!
　　The nobles all requested then
Safe conduct back to their homes again.
To them Sir Asprian replied:
4900 "Why don't you all begin to ride?
If anyone is set upon,
I'll hurry to his aid anon."
The giant Widolt said thereto:
"I promise to succor all of you
4905 Who have sworn to Rother fealty:
You surely can depend on me!
Whenever I hear of someone's need,
I'll come to his aid with all possible speed."
Then Asprian's followers let it be known
4910 That they would not remain at home
If it were ever to happen again
That Rother should be needing them.
"Whoever tries to injure him
We'll tear like a chicken limb from limb!"
　　　… … … … … … … … … … …
4915 Both to envy and to sneer
Almighty God forbade us here.
And so it was in the whole domain
As long as the mighty Rother reigned.
If one was guilty of such a sin,
4920 His life was taken away from him.
Hence it was known to every man —
Both at the court and on the land —
That whoso pledged aught to anyone
Would surely see that it was done,
4925 Provided he did not die before
Or be prevented by the law.
　　Rother honored with a kiss —
What pleasure he derived from this! —
Many a worthy man that day.
4930 Then they saddled the horses without delay.
　　　… … … … … … … … … … …
Back to their homelands once again.
Then before the king there rode a knight
Upon a courser shining bright.
In gleaming armor he rode his way,

L. 4914 Several lines seem to have been omitted here.
L. 4930 A line is missing here.

4935 Well-equipped for any fray.
Upon his legs the hero bold
Was wearing greaves encased in gold,
In which there had been set with skill
Gems to make them fairer still.
4940 Upon his shield there could be seen
An animal with a playful mien.
It had been wrought of the finest gold
And looked like a dragon, so we're told.
And set around it in artful wise
4945 Were stones both great and small in size
Which cast abroad a radiant light
Like stars a-shining in the night.
All around the shield's rim
Precious sapphires were set in.
4950 Upon the hero's saddle-bow
Golden swans stood in a row.
Upon his helmet was a stone
Which at the hour of midnight shone
In such a very dazzling way
4955 That one might think it was bright day.
(Alexander, the mighty man,
Had brought it back from a foreign land
Where Christian folk had never been
Either before or after him.)
4960   The stone was named Claugestian;
It adorned the helm of an ancient man.
His beard was very long indeed.
How fearlessly he rode his steed!
It galloped for him, in very truth,
4965 Better than for any youth.
Rother bade the knight farewell.
It was Duke Berchter, so we hear tell,
For the sake of whom his wife so dear
Had shed at home full many a tear.
4970 (Later at our Lord's command
He came home safely to his land.)
   As soon as Berchter did receive
The king's permission for him to leave,
Then off he rode with a mighty throng.
4975 They raised their voices high in song
As on their steeds they rode along.
Many a lady had to stare
As they went riding away from there.
Rother hated to see them go.

4980 "Ah, how heavy is this blow!
Assurance to the world I give
That just as long as I shall live,
My pleasure it will be to share —
Like the eagle of the air —
4985 All that I possess of treasure
With rich and poor in equal measure,
Whenever it is asked of me
And one shall seek it honorably —
As long as a loaf is mine to spend."
4990 Asprian and Widolt then
Along with Rother's other men
Journeyed homeward once again.
An honest course they did pursue,
Esteemed by everyone — that is true!
4995 The years that passed were twenty-two.
By then had Pippin become a man
So that he was fit to rule the land.
Truly, the noble Rother had
Very honestly reared the lad —
5000 Just as today still many a man
Raises his son as best he can.
Rother dwelled in his domain
(The Lord had spared him every pain)
And raised the youthful Pippin
5005 (He was a son most dear to him)
In splendid fashion, so we're told,
Till he was twenty-four years old.
Thereupon the youth implored
That he be knighted with the sword.
5010 At Aachen then one did convoke
A great assembly of the folk,
To which full many a worthy knight
Came as splendidly as he might.
They rode to the court from far and near,
5015 Each in the company of his peer.
To the court there rode full many a lord
The time that Pippin received the sword.
Thither came Sir Asprian
Along with Widolt, the valiant man.
5020 The hero Grimme came there too
(He belonged to the giants' retinue

L. 4984 *the eagle* — a symbol of generosity; it was supposed to leave some of its prey for other birds to devour.

And was indeed a gruesome lad.)
Attending him Sir Asprian had
Warriors seven hundred strong.
5025 They carried iron clubs along.
    Then at the head of a handsome band
There rode across the Frankish land
To Rother's court a valiant youth.
'Twas Wolfrat of Tengeling, in truth,
5030 Leading doughty warriors there.
Thirty thousand heroes fair
Traveled under his command
For the assembly of the land.
From the land of Spain did Erwin ride
5035 With Master Lupold at his side.
Both were men of high degree
And traveled with propriety.
The faithful Lupold led, we're told,
Sixty thousand heroes bold
5040 From the kingdom of the Franks
That he might merit Pippin's thanks.
Ah, how Rother rejoiced aloud
When he caught sight of these heroes proud.
    At Aachen they stayed overnight
5045 Until the morning showed its light.
As soon as the day began to break,
Upon his horse was seen to wait
The youthful Pippin, a hero bold,
Splendidly adorned with gold.
5050 The coursers started galloping then
Underneath the youthful men.
Into the melee rode many a lord
The time that Pippin received the sword.
Widolt and Grimme began to race
5055 All around the ring apace.
Such a noise did the giants make
That all the ground began to shake.
At Aachen then the feast went on
Until three days had come and gone.
5060 Homeward then prepared to fare
All who had assembled there.
Then Pippin vowed to every man
That he would confirm him in his land
After the mighty Rother died
5065 And he ruled over the countryside.
    The festival had reached an end.

Then every man began to wend
Homeward to his own domain.
There they resided free from blame.
5070 The noble Rother spent his days
In a way that earned him the highest praise.
　　As soon as Pippin, the youthful lord,
Had been presented with the sword
There in the Emperor Rother's sight,
5075 He rode through the land with many a knight
And judged according to the law
Lord and vassal as heretofore.
So at Aachen did disband
The great assembly of the land.
5080 　　Across the land came hurrying there
A warrior with snow-white hair —
For which old age must take the blame.
Riding close behind him came
Two thousand heroes unafeared.
5085 Around his ears had all been sheared
The noble hair upon his head.
In all respects he had been bred
To be the very truest man
Who ever served at a king's right hand.
5090 To Aachen he had set out riding
As soon as he received the tiding.
His horse's reins he firmly grasped.
How very little time elapsed
Ere Rother caught a glimpse of him!
5095 Now hear the words of the mighty king:
"In truth, I am a happy man:
Here comes the hero of Meran!
Welcome him with courteous mien."
"I'll gladly do so," said the queen.
5100 Verily, she was not remiss:
She honored the good duke with a kiss.
The noble Rother could hardly wait
Till Berchter had ridden through the gate.
With his very own hand he held his steed:
5105 The hero had merited this indeed!
Then Rother's followers did the same:
They saluted those who with Berchter came.
In this way did the honest men
Only do what befitted them,
5110 Because the valiant hero had
Proved himself a valiant lad

When he had still been in his prime
And had ridden to battle many a time.
As soon as the noble duke had heard
5115 Everything that had occurred,
Then he began without more ado
To counsel Rother what to do.
"Join with me, O worthy man,
In the execution of my plan
5120 And help thereby your wretched soul —
Of an honest life that is the goal.
My lord, your hair is turning grey.
Everything must pass away.
All good men it does become,
5125 When their life is almost done,
To make their peace with God on high
Before the hour when they must die.
Here in the world you won much fame.
Of my companions there once came
5130 Sixteen to a rendezvous
And considered what they ought to do.
They shed, dear master, many a tear
Because for your father the end was near.
In Death's grip lay the hero true
5135 And bade that I look after you.
Since then I've never left your side,
So that nobody ever tried
To do you any injury
Without at the same time threatening me.
5140 What I say now, dear sir, is true:
I can only be of help to you
If to my counsel you pay heed.
In that event you will be freed
Forevermore of every dole —
5145 And you will benefit your soul!"
   The mighty king sat silent then.
Berchter spoke to him again:
"Noble lord, my words are true:
It's good advice I'm offering you.
5150 Deserve of the saints their mediation.
Wealth is an abomination!
Here on earth it is unclean;
In our heavenly home it can't be seen.
However much a man may win,
5155 How quickly it gets away from him —
As we can notice every day.

Follow my advice, I pray,
  And help your wretched soul thereby,
  That it may live and never die.
5160 There is no need to be distressed.
  Whosoever has been blessed
  With the grace of Christ our Heavenly King
  Will cherish it more than anything.
  There was no limit to your might.
5165 For you went everything just right.
  What does that come to anyhow?
  If someone should surpass you now,
  To him you then must needs defer.
  Now heed my counsel, gracious sir:
5170 Let us both to Fulda wend.
  Whoever seeks a blessed end
  May gladly don there monks' attire.
  Let both of us be monks, dear sire!
  To our poor souls we must pay heed.
5175 Inconstant is this life we lead!"
  Then answered him the worthy king
  That he would gladly do this thing.
     Rother did not linger there:
  He hurried to his lady fair
5180 And told her what he meant to do.
  The goodly queen replied thereto:
  "Berchter never has, I vow,
  Counseled better than he has now.
  O noble Rother, do his will!
5185 It surely will not turn out ill."
  Then said the … … … … … … … …
  … … … … … … … … … … … …
  Just as it still today does stand,
  So that it is honored throughout the land.
  Then from the world the queen withdrew,
5190 As God Almighty inspired her to.
  Then throughout all the Roman land
  Peace prevailed on every hand
  Until King Pippin passed away
  And over the empire Karl held sway.
5195 A splendid lord he proved to be,
  And he ruled the land most prudently.
  Now to an end our tale has come.
  Fold your hands now everyone

   L. 5186 A number of lines have been omitted here.

And pray to Almighty God on high,
5200 Who fashioned us to live and die,
That to the poet He show His grace
And keep you also … … … … … … … …

UNIVERSITY OF NORTH CAROLINA STUDIES IN THE GERMANIC LANGUAGES AND LITERATURES

Publication Committee

FREDERIC E. COENEN, EDITOR

WERNER P. FRIEDERICH GEORGE S. LANE
JOHN G. KUNSTMANN HERBERT W. REICHERT

1. Herbert W. Reichert. THE BASIC CONCEPTS IN THE PHILOSOPHY OF GOTTFRIED KELLER. 1949. Pp. 164. Paper $ 3.00. Out of print.
2. Olga Marx and Ernst Morwitz. THE WORKS OF STEFAN GEORGE. Rendered into English. 1949. Out of print.
3. Paul H. Curts. HEROD AND MARIAMNE, A Tragedy in Five Acts by Friedrich Hebbel, Translated into English Verse. 1950. Pp. 96. Cloth $ 3.00.
4. Frederic E. Coenen. FRANZ GRILLPARZER'S PORTRAITURE OF MEN. 1951. Pp xii, 135. Cloth $ 3.50.
5. Edwin H. Zeydel and B. Q. Morgan. THE PARZIVAL OF WOLFRAM VON ESCHENBACH. Translated into English Verse, with Introductions, Notes, and Connecting Summaries. 1951, 1956, 1960, Pp. xii, 370. Paper $ 4.50.
6. James C. O'Flaherty. UNITY AND LANGUAGE: A STUDY IN THE PHILOSOPHY OF JOHANN GEORG HAMANN. 1952. Out of print.
7. Sten G. Flygt. FRIEDRICH HEBBEL'S CONCEPTION OF MOVEMENT IN THE ABSOLUTE AND IN HISTORY. 1952. Out of print.
8. Richard Kuehnemund. ARMINIUS OR THE RISE OF A NATIONAL SYMBOL. (From Hutten to Grabbe.) 1953. Pp. xxx. 122, Cloth $ 3.50.
9. Lawrence S. Thompson. WILHELM WAIBLINGER IN ITALY. 1953. Pp. ix. 105. Paper $ 3.00.
10. Frederick Hiebel. NOVALIS. GERMAN POET - EUROPEAN THINKER - CHRISTIAN MYSTIC. 1953. Pp. xii, 126. 2nd rev. ed. 1959. Paper $ 3.50.

(2) bro 7/6/67